BLUEPRINT FOR LARCENY

They made ill-assorted company — the voluptuous girl who called herself Toni Graham, the youth named Tip Brennan . . . and Benedict. The girl did not like Benedict. He had hard eyes that looked at her without desire but seemed to probe her mind instead. Tip didn't like him either, although he knew a big operator when he saw one and was eager enough to graduate from petty crime to the really big take. No, it was the money they liked. The bait that Benedict held out to them . . .

PETER CHESTER

BLUEPRINT FOR LARCENY

Complete and Unabridged

LINFORD
Leicester

First published in Great Britain in 1964

published 2003

All the characters in this book are
purely imaginary and have no relation
whatsoever to any living persons.

British Library CIP Data

Chester, Peter, *1924* –
    Blueprint for larceny—Large print ed.—
    Linford mystery library
    1. Detective and mystery stories
    2. Large type books
    I. Title
    823.9'14 [F]

    ISBN 0–7089–9968–9

Published by
F. A. Thorpe (Publishing)
Anstey, Leicestershire

Set by Words & Graphics Ltd.
Anstey, Leicestershire
Printed and bound in Great Britain by
T. J. International Ltd., Padstow, Cornwall

This book is printed on acid-free paper

For Alexandra

1

The wet, black ribbon of the road unwound endlessly under the yellow probing of the headlights. Mile after mile was swallowed up and disappeared into the rain-sodden darkness behind. The man at the wheel stared unblinkingly through the hazy windshield, while the monotonous rhythm of the wipers battled sullenly with the driving rain.

The road took an upward curve and there suddenly was the town below, a neon oasis in the gloom.

The driver glanced quickly at the illuminated clock on the dash and noted that he'd accomplished the sixty-mile trip within four minutes of the time he'd scheduled. He could have been pleased, even secretly slightly proud of being so close to his estimate. Another man could have been. Would have. But this was not any other man. This one merely noted the fact.

He was passing through the fringe of town now, picking up some company by way of traffic. He drove well, always allowing little courtesies to others who felt entitled to a share of the road. Even more than their share. Finally, at a busy intersection he turned off right, nosing his way into a quarter of the city where the lights were noisier, more aggressive. More scattered too, like vulgar chattering islands dotted along the dim and somehow ominous streets. He pulled into the kerb and eased on the brakes.

The place he wanted was on the opposite side of the street. A sign flashed intermittently against the damp sky, announcing that this was Eddie's. At street level, neon tubing framed a doorway, but no other lights showed through the thick curtaining at the door and windows.

A few yards away three boys lounged in a doorway. They wore jackets of black leather and daubed on each was a crude outline of a space rocket. They'd noted the big sedan, noted the out-of-town plates. The guy was going to Eddie's, that

2

much was clear, and Eddie's being what it was, the guy may be quite some time in there. Since he was from out-of-town he could be some slob just looking for a little action around the bright lights. And when you have a slob leaving a fine big sedan parked outside Eddie's on a dark night, you have a situation which could be turned to some advantage. Especially by smart apples with space rockets on their coats.

The car door slammed shut as the driver heaved himself out on the sidewalk.

'Here he comes now.'

'Yeah, he didn't even lock it. What a sucker.'

'Shut up.'

All three fell to an intense study of their hands, one boy scraping away meticulously at his finger-nails with a pocket-knife. From the corners of their eyes they watched the driver cross the street. He was a big guy, they noted. Why wasn't he going into Eddie's? Where did he think he was going? Jeez, he's walking right up to us. He's —

'You.'

The big man stood in front of them, jabbing a finger at the nearest boy. The boy looked up, studied him insolently, then resumed the art work on his finger nails. The man chuckled. Then with an easy, almost graceful movement, he grasped hold of the front of the leather jacket with both hands. Seemingly without effort he lifted the boy and banged him hard against the wall. The pocket-knife clattered to the ground, while the kid shook himself and stared hate at the aggressor.

'Hey, whassa big — ' began one of the others.

'Shut up.'

The man let go and put his hands casually into his pockets.

'This your turf?' he demanded.

All three nodded. This was no slob. This was a guy who walked right up to three of them, pushed one around, then calmly stuck his hands in his pockets. As though they weren't there. This was the big time. And get a load of that suit.

'O.K. I gotta rule. Never interfere with the local businessmen. This is your turf.

Over there,' he jerked a thumb, 'that's my car. It's parked on your territory, so all right. Here, rental fee.'

He pulled out a bulging pigskin billfold, making no attempt to hide the thick wad of notes. Carefully he extracted a five-dollar bill and handed it to the nearest boy. At the last moment he grabbed the outstretched hand and squeezed the extended fingers. The boy gasped with sudden pain.

'Anything happens to that car, even just a little old bitty scratch on the paintwork, I look for you. Ketch?'

The boy nodded again.

'Ketch.'

The man turned his back contemptuously and walked to the illuminated entrance.

'Boy, if that guy's looking for somebody in that joint, I'm glad I'm out here,' breathed one boy.

The one with the bruised fingers stood rubbing his hand and cursing.

The big man opened the door and stepped inside. Eddie's was nothing spectacular. Just a bar, with some carpets and soft lighting and maybe a girl to help you spend your money. The place was quietly busy, twenty or so drinkers scattered around the small tables, two more of the really thirsty perched at the bar itself where it wasn't such a long time between drinks. The barkeep was a small Spanish-looking man with a black polished head and pencil-line moustache to match. His eyes flicked over the newcomer knowingly. The barman wasn't a teenager in a leather jacket. He was a forty year old in a white tuxedo, and he'd looked at a lot of people across a lot of bars. Already he knew two things about his latest customer, he hadn't come there to drink and he hadn't come because he was lonely. A man like him didn't have to buy liquor on percentage in order to get a woman to sit with him. Plenty would be glad of the chance. The man behind the bar glanced casually into one corner of the room and raised his eyebrows.

In the corner a big, brutish-looking character caught the glance and nodded to show he'd seen the newcomer. The man in the corner spent his working life catching and interpreting glances of various kinds. Every now and then he'd have to lumber up from his comfortable seat and make noises like a bouncer. More than noises if the troublemaker couldn't take a hint, but usually one look at the ape-like figure with the thick knotted hands was enough to convince the opposition. The bouncer's name was Sam, and he didn't really like trouble. What he liked was sitting quietly in his corner, admiring the girls who worked the place, and reflecting sadly on the bad luck which had deprived him of a crack at the heavyweight title years before.

The swarthy bartender made a great display of polishing at the slender-stemmed glass in his hand. He even pretended to look slightly startled to find a new customer was waiting for service.

'What'll it be, sir?'

'Go and tell Eddie I'm here.'

The customer didn't sit on the tall padded stools and he didn't lean on the bar. Just stood and waited for the man behind it to go and do as he was told. He didn't miss the quickly elevated eyebrows, which quickly brought a new voice breathing gently close to his ear.

'You want exactly what?' queried Sam.

'Eddie.' The customer didn't even turn round. 'Go tell him I'm here.'

Sam was puzzled. People had all kinds of reactions to Sam. They got scared or aggressive, they blustered or they whined. One thing they never did was stand with their backs to him and give him orders. When anything out of the ordinary happened, Sam always had to pause while he reasoned it through. He was still no more than halfway to a solution when the bartender said,

'Tell him who's here? I never saw you before.'

'Just tell him, that's all. Say it's the guy he's expecting.'

The barman hesitated, looked again at the pale blue eyes that stared at him unwinking.

'Okay, Sam, do like he says.'

'Huh?'

Sam was still puzzled.

'Go tell the boss, Sam,' said the barman gently. 'Say there's a guy out here says he's expected.'

Sam nodded. Cliff the barman was a good guy. If he said okay, okay. The bouncer nodded again and shambled away to a curtained opening in the side wall.

Cliff got on with his routine of polishing and generally looking busy. The customer had turned his back to the bar now and Cliff studied him covertly as he worked. In his own mind he was hoping Eddie hadn't done anything foolish, such as overlooking any of the heavy kickbacks which were essential to keeping the place open without trouble. This big man with the cold eyes may or may not be trouble, but he could be. Cliff had been behind a lot of bars for almost a quarter of a century and he knew what kind of wrapping trouble came in.

Sam was back in less than a minute. Ignoring the visitor he said hoarsely to Cliff:

'Boss says O.K.'

'All right, Sam.' Cliff let his voice be just loud enough for the stranger to hear. 'Take him in to the office. And Sam, better stick around in case Mr. Rugolo wants you for anything.'

Sam wagged his great head up and down then went back the way he'd come. The stranger tagged along behind. There was a narrow passage on the other side of the curtain. Sam opened a door.

'In here.'

The big man stepped through into a small room. There was carpet on the floor and a small leather-topped desk. Behind it sat a small, neat man with black oily hair and a pale watchful face. He looked carefully at his visitor and nodded.

'Beat it, Sam.'

Sam glanced at each man uncertainly, then shrugged his great shoulders and shuffled out.

'You're Rugolo,' said the big man flatly. It was not a question but a plain statement of fact.

'I'm Rugolo,' agreed the other. 'Do you have a name or is that none of my business either?'

'Lots of names, all kinds. This week I'm Benedict.'

'You wanta sit down?'

The club-owner was ill at ease. He didn't like Benedict, didn't like the people who sent him. What Rugolo did like was the fat easy life that came from running Eddie's, and the only way to guarantee that he stayed in business was to do as he was told when people like Benedict turned up.

Benedict had parked himself on a hardback chair facing the door and with a wall behind him.

'Did you tell her anything?'

'Tell who?' retorted the man at the desk. 'I don't even know which one it is.'

'Good.'

Benedict took a pack of cigarettes from a side pocket and lit one.

'It's the blonde. Calls herself Toni Graham.'

Rugolo assimilated this piece of information carefully. Then he said:

'The deal I got was she don't have to go if she don't want to. All I guarantee is to produce her. If she don't wanta buy, it's no sale, and no hard feelings. That right?'

Benedict nodded, blue smoke curling lazily from his nostrils.

'And you keep the job open while she's away,' he added.

'Well, now, that's not too easy,' protested the club-owner. 'You drag off one of my girls to God-knows-where. Maybe she'll come back and maybe she won't. This is a business I'm running here. I gotta have just so many girls peddling out there — '

His voice tailed away as Benedict slewed round to face him.

'The job stays open. Don't make it tough on yourself, Rugolo. You're not built for that kind of work. Get her in here.'

Rugolo shrugged and pushed at a button at the edge of his desk. Almost at once the barman, Cliff, came in on the run, hand jammed down into his pocket. When he saw the two men sitting calmly waiting, he stopped, flustered.

'Tell the Graham girl I wanta see her,' barked his boss. 'Don't tell her anything else. Just that.'

Cliff turned and went out.

12

'What's his name, the bar jockey?' queried Benedict.

'He didn't mean no harm, Benedict. He was just — '

'Running round after you is what he was just,' interrupted Benedict. 'The name.'

'Lepeski, Cliff Lepeski.'

'He's O.K.,' nodded Benedict. 'I'll remember him.'

Rugolo didn't want to talk about Cliff. He had something else on his mind.

'My end of this is two and a half C's,' he said pointedly.

'You'll get it,' assured the other.

'Suppose she turns it down? What's to stop you just walking out?'

Benedict sighed and produced the stuffed billfold. He extracted two one hundred dollar bills and a fifty. Then he tossed the money contemptuously on the table.

'Cheap,' he sneered. 'You're a cheap little man, Rugolo. Cheap little joint, cheap little man.'

Rugolo went very white but he said nothing. There was a knock at the door and Cliff put his head in.

'Here she is, boss.'

Benedict lost interest in Rugolo and turned his pale blue gaze towards the girl who was framed in the doorway.

2

She was slightly above medium height, about five feet six inches. She had brown eyes and high cheekbones, a face that was thoughtful rather than pretty. A good clean line to her jaw, and a wide generous mouth that was too large for symmetry. The fine golden hair was piled up on top, accentuating the length of her face. She wore a dress of red silk that looked as if it had been moulded straight on to the voluptuous curving body. Toni Graham could not be called beautiful, but she was certainly striking.

She was wondering what Mr. Rugolo wanted. The boss didn't very often call anybody in to his office. Wondering too who the other man was, the big stranger with the muscled body and the cold stare.

'C'm on in, honey,' Rugolo said in a friendly tone. 'Cliff, shut that door and see nobody comes in.'

The girl stepped further into the room

and the door closed firmly behind her. Rugolo got up. He didn't like this, and all he wanted was to get it over with and get this cold fish Benedict out of his place.

'Look, baby,' he smiled nervously. 'This is a friend of mine. He has something he wants to talk to you about. I'll just step outside for a few minutes. It's kind of confidential.'

She caught the apprehension in his voice and wondered. Rugolo was a name in town, and yet this so-called friend obviously gave him the jitters. It made her curious, just as much as what he'd said about this friend wanting to talk to her. What about?

'What's it all about, Mr. Rugolo?'

'Well, now, baby — ' began Rugolo.

'Beat it,' snapped Benedict. 'You've filled your end. Wait outside.'

Rugolo nodded unhappily, and was obviously relieved to go.

'What'd you do to him?' queried the girl.

'Sit down,' ordered the big man.

She shrugged and did as she was told. The red silk rode up as she sat and she arranged the skirt carefully, in such a way as to look tidy without concealing too much of the long beautiful legs.

'And you can put those away,' said Benedict shortly. 'I've seen plenty better and we're here to talk business.'

This was a strange man indeed, she reflected. Not that there was anything wrong with his reflexes. She'd noted the quick interest in his eyes when she first came into the room. Almost shyly, she pushed her skirt down to a less revealing level.

'Mister, I don't know who you are — ' she began.

'Just shut up and listen,' he snapped. 'You can talk after you've heard what I have to say. O.K.?'

She shrugged.

'O.K.'

Whatever this guy wanted it was making a break from being slobbered over by those crums outside. The nightly stint of dodging the sidling hands could take it out of a girl, and this interlude was a welcome relief. Depending on what lay at the end, of course.

'You call yourself Toni Graham. You told Rugolo you're twenty-three years old and you come from Ohio. Your real name is Trudi Buckman, you took three years off your age, and you're from San Antonio, Texas.'

She caught her breath. Now she was afraid. Now she wished she was back outside with the slobs. That was only dirty and unpleasant. This man was dangerous. Very dangerous. Finally she found her voice.

'Who — where did you — ?'

'Never mind that now. Your brother's in jail down there and he's going to draw thirty years if you don't help him. Helping him means hiring a real big legal name. That takes money, and you haven't got it.'

'What are you, some kind of policeman?' she blurted out.

Benedict shook his head.

'No policeman. Just a man whose business it is to know things about people. Things that can help me. I've got a proposition for you. You hear it out, you say yes or no. Here, tonight. There's no second bids. If you're in, you're all the way in. Ketch?'

Suddenly she felt cold. There were chill fingers clawing at her spine. It was this man, there was something cold yet compelling about him. Not like a snake exactly, but — something. Too, she wondered what was meant by 'all the way in.'

'This proposition,' she said haltingly. 'Do I get to ask any questions?'

'Many as you like. I don't guarantee answers, but if I do answer, what you'll hear will be the truth.'

She believed him. This was no cheapskate and no loudmouth either. He was probably other things, worse things, but not those.

'It's your deal,' she told him.

'Here it is. I want you to come with me for three or four days. There's a thing I'm working on and I can use you. You may have to risk your neck, but I doubt it. Not the way I've worked it out. If I'm not satisfied it's gonna be safe, nothing happens, we scrap the whole caper. If we do, I bring you back here. Rugolo's keeping your job warm, and I'll pay you a hundred dollars a day for the time out.'

A hundred a day. And for doing nothing. Well, maybe not entirely nothing, Toni reflected. After all, for that kind of money this big man might feel he was entitled to a little extra service. And at those prices he would get it.

'No questions yet?' he demanded, after a pause.

'I'll hear the rest of it first.'

He didn't smile exactly, but the corners of his mouth quirked slightly for an instant.

'If we pull it off, this thing I have in mind, your end will be ten thousand dollars, less whatever I stake you now.'

Just like that. Ten grand. Why, with a sum like that she could — well, do anything. Everything. Including getting that no-good brother off the hook.

'T-ten thousand?' she faltered.

Benedict did smile this time, only it was thin and without humour.

'Less whatever I stake you,' he reminded.

He'd been through interviews like this

too often in the past. When they started out, the amateurs, they all got those big saucer eyes when they first heard their share of the take. He always made sure they had a fair offer for whatever they had to do. But sooner or later most of them got greedy. They'd start thinking about the haul, and what their end would be, and how it wasn't fair they didn't get as much as this one or that one. Or Benedict, even. Benedict who dreamed up the whole deal, spent weeks or even months ironing out the wrinkles, so there was a maximum chance of success. So that all they had to do was follow simple instructions and get paid more money than they'd ever dreamed of. They even looked greedily at Benedict's share sometimes. Only he would be ready for that. He was always ready for everything. He sat now, smiling that mirthless smile, and watching the amazement, the cupidity, the doubt, all struggling for supremacy in the girl's expression. There was little doubt in his mind that she'd go for it. But if not, it wouldn't matter. There

21

were already alternative arrangements planned.

Toni was watching him too as the thoughts tumbled over each other in her mind. Not that there was any doubt about her ultimate reply, she knew that. Knew, too, that he knew it, that big grinning devil. Playing with her, that's what he was doing. He knew damned well she'd accept in the end. Well, it never pays a girl to look too anxious.

'Question time?' she enquired.

'Go ahead.'

'How do I know this isn't just a big pitch?' she demanded. 'How do I know you're not just going to drive me out in the desert and cut me up? You could be a sex-killer, for all I know.'

He didn't get mad, or even flustered. On the contrary, he was amused.

'Well, well,' he grinned. 'Every day something new. Tell you this, honey, nobody ever thought up that one before. But it's a fair question. Take a look at me. I'm nobody's Rock Hudson, but if I ever want a woman I can usually get one. Through the normal procedure, I mean.

Anyway, don't take my word. Ask Rugolo. He's all kind of things, but he doesn't let his girls wander off with guys like that. And he does know me.'

She nodded. He was right, of course. She'd never seriously thought there was anything wrong with him. With those other guys, the creeps, she could always tell. She was afraid of this man, but that wasn't the reason. And, as he said, she could ask Mr. Rugolo.

'I'll ask him,' she replied. 'This thing you want me to do, it has to be crooked.'

'It's crooked,' he acknowledged.

'Is — is anybody going to get killed?'

This was the question she was afraid of. There had to be a chance of murder where this kind of money was involved. Toni was afraid of murder and had to ask. But she didn't want him to admit it, didn't want him to take away that golden prospect of the ten grand. Say no, she whispered inside herself, please say no. Lie to me, if you have to, but say no.

He looked at her steadily before replying. Then he said:

'The way I've mapped it out there

shouldn't be any violence. But we'll have to be prepared for it, if it happens. If I were making a book, I'd say the price would be three to one against.'

Well, those were good odds. That didn't sound too bad. It meant there'd probably be no shooting at all. Anyway, if it did come to shooting, that didn't have to mean death, did it? Plenty of places you could get wounded. Like in the shoulder, or the leg maybe. Didn't have to be fatal, did it? Three to one against any shooting. That was pretty good, specially when you added up the extra odds against anybody getting killed even if there were any.

'That's a straight answer,' she mumbled. 'When does all this start?'

'If you're in, it already started,' he informed her. 'We'll leave here together the minute we're through talking.'

Something like panic flew into her mind.

'Oh no, I couldn't do that. Not just walk out like that. People would wonder where I was.'

'Rugolo'll tell 'em,' he returned dispassionately. 'Just give him the names. He'll say you've been called away to a sick relative.'

'But my clothes,' she stammered, 'I can't wear this thing out on the street.'

'Buy new ones. I'll give you money.'

'What about my apartment?' she said desperately. This deal was crowding in too suddenly, pushing her, forcing her. There wasn't any time to think it over properly.

As though he could see into her mind, he whispered:

'What's the objection? There's nothing to think about, is there? Either you want the money or you don't. Just like that.'

Just like that, she thought bitterly. You don't just go walking out into the night with a perfect stranger, to go rushing off God alone knows where. With just one dress to see you through three or four days. For ten thousand dollars, she remembered. For ten thousand dollars, you do whatever's needed, whatever you're told. This was that one time when you heard that knocking at the door. If you didn't answer it, it would never happen again. Ten thousand dollars. She took a deep breath and closed her eyes.

'All right,' she sighed.

'You're in?' he demanded.

'I'm in.'

Benedict nodded, satisfied. He was glad the girl agreed. He'd spent some time looking over likely girls and of the three he finally selected, this was the one who'd do the job best. And he was quite certain she could and would do it when the time came. Walking across to the door he opened it and looked out. Rugolo was across the passage leaning against the wall, smoking a cigarette.

'C'm in,' invited Benedict.

Rugolo lounged up from the wall. He didn't like being invited into his own office. He didn't like being told what to do. He didn't like this guy taking his best girl off God-knew-where just when business was brisk. But he didn't say anything, didn't even show his thoughts on his face. Because there were certain things Rugolo did like. Things like two hundred and fifty dollars for doing nothing. Like having the good word with the big men upstate. He also liked his features the way they were, and not all scrambled up the way they'd be if he annoyed this big quiet visitor.

Forcing a grin, Rugolo walked into the office.

'Well, how'd it go?' he enquired.

'We're leaving,' Benedict told him. Then to the girl, 'You got a purse or a coat here?'

She started to get up.

'Yeah, they're outside. I'll — '

'Sit down,' ordered Benedict. 'Have somebody get 'em for her, Rugolo. From here on, she stays with me.'

Rugolo shrugged.

'I don't have anybody out there right this minute.'

The big man turned towards him, the pale eyes almost translucent.

'Well?'

The club-owner opened his mouth to say something, changed his mind and shrugged again. Then, with tight lips, he turned and went out.

Toni watched this performance with astonishment. Boy, if some of that crowd out there could have seen that. Seen the way this big guy sent Mr. Rugolo off on an errand for him. Just like that. And him, Rugolo, not even arguing about it. This big fellow, this Benedict, he was something all right. Around Eddie's, when Mr. Rugolo said jump, you jumped, if you knew what time it was. But this other one, he just talked to Mr. Rugolo like he was a car-hop or something.

'Where we going, Mr. Benedict?' she ventured.

For a long moment he made no reply. Then he said, very slowly and distinctly.

'One thing we have to get straight at the start. When I want you to know anything, I'll tell you. I'll tell you when to eat, and when to sleep. When to talk, and when to clam up. You're on my time now, remember it.'

She nodded uneasily. If he wasn't going to loosen up at all, it looked like being a cheerful three or four days. A real ball. Then she thought about the money again, and that better than evened things up.

Rugolo was soon back, a lightweight coat across his arm and a red purse flashing with silver sequins in his hand. These he thrust ungraciously at Toni.

'Anything else?' he demanded. When he started to speak he'd meant to sound aggressive, but somehow the force oozed out of the words just as they left his mouth. They ended as a plain question.

Benedict shook his head.

'We're leaving now. You fix things this end, so nobody wonders where she's gone. Oh yes, there is one thing.'

Rugolo cocked his head to one side and waited.

'She wants you to tell her whether I'm a sex-killer.'

Despite his annoyance, Rugolo could not resist a chuckle.

'Not lately' he grinned. 'You more or less gave that up, didn't you, since you cut the heads off those four women up in Maine last year?'

Toni smiled sheepishly and stared at the floor. Benedict went to the door.

'We'll use your side entrance,' he said curtly. 'C'mon.'

She followed him out, nodding a farewell to Rugolo, who didn't move.

3

A side entrance to a place like Eddie's needs two main characteristics. A minimum of light and plenty of oil on the hinges. People using the side door did not, as a rule, wish to find themselves in a sudden blaze of light; and as for the oil, well, a door that squeaks is about as private as a brass-band concert. The hinges eased smoothly back as Benedict swung the door open a foot. The girl looked out at the rain-slicked concrete without enthusiasm. She couldn't see why they didn't walk out the front entrance. Presumably this cold man had a car out here somewhere, so why not get as near to it as possible without having to track through all this wet. That was what she was thinking, but already she knew better than to say anything. This guy said he was calling the shots, and that didn't mean he wanted any chatter about which door to use.

Benedict stuck his head through the opening, and peered round towards the front of the place. Then he pulled back inside quickly.

'Stay close behind me. If you make any noise, any noise at all, I'll kick your teeth in. Savvy?'

It was less the words themselves than the conversational tone in which they were delivered which frightened the girl more. She nodded vigorously to show she understood. He nodded once then slipped out, melting into the wet gloom at the side of the building. Toni followed, shivering slightly as the first cold rainspots hit her. It was then she saw the reason for the silence, saw the three figures huddled together at the corner of the street. Silent watchful figures, part of the night, oblivious to everything but the anticipation of an unsuspecting man who would step out from Eddie's garish entrance.

Fascinated, Toni watched Benedict as he inched forward, silently closing the twenty foot gap. Now he was not more than four feet behind the nearest of the watchers. His hand moved to his pocket, and when it emerged there was something in it. He took a step forward and held the something against the neck of the man in front.

'You boys looking for something?' he asked gently.

The others swung round, but the one who could feel the cold muzzle of the gun at his neck was frozen in fear. The others hesitated. Benedict chuckled.

'C'mon, you guys, let's have a little fun. Step back here.'

They still hesitated, looking at each other uncertainly.

'For crissakes, fellers, give me a break. This guy'll kill me.'

Slowly the two came forward.

'Well, well,' muttered Benedict. 'You're kind of rough company, huh? Brass knuckles, you. And what's buddy boy here got? A knife. And what about you, Happy? Where's yours?'

The kid on the other end of the gun shook his head.

'Nothin', honest. Nothin'.'

Benedict punched him in the kidneys, not too hard.

'Try again,' he invited.

'It's, it's in my pocket,' breathed the other painfully.

'Well, come on, everybody's showing out. It's a party. Get it. Or shall I — ?'

'No, no.'

The kid dived in the front of his jacket and held a knife up in his hand.

'That's better,' grunted Benedict. 'More friendly. I've always been a friendly guy. You were going to have a little fun. Don't let me stop you.'

'Huh?'

Toni was spread against the wall, watching with terrified fascination. Benedict pushed the boy forward till he was no more than a foot away from his companions.

'Go ahead,' he ordered. 'Stick somebody.'

'Listen mister — ,' whined one.

'Shut up.'

Benedict kicked lightly at the back of his victim's knee.

'Stick somebody.'

He moved round, so that all three could see the heavy ugliness of the weapon in his hand.

'This guy is nuts,' snarled the kid with the brass knuckles. 'I'm getting outa here.'

The other two never saw the big man move, but suddenly the big automatic swung sickeningly against the side of the speaker's head. He fell against the wall, face scraping against the brickwork as he slid down.

'Now I'm getting impatient,' snapped Benedict. 'Let's see some action.'

The two stood staring at their crumpled companion.

'He's dead,' whispered one.

'Maybe,' shrugged Benedict. 'You wanta try it, or would you sooner fight Happy here?'

There was no argument now. Both the boys realised it at the same moment. This guy was a candidate for a strait-jacket. If they didn't fight, they'd wind up face down on the concrete too. Suddenly one boy struck out, the knife blade gleaming dully in the rain. The other jumped back quickly but the slicing blade ripped at the front of his jacket. Toni moved rapidly out into the open and went to stand beside Benedict.

'You've gotta stop this,' she hissed. 'This is murder.'

'I'm not doing anything,' returned the big man evenly. 'These kids wanta fight it's their business.'

She watched horrified as the two circled warily, feinting all the time with their knife-hands. One lunged forward, missed, and as his blade flashed harmlessly past the dodging shoulder, the other kid jabbed viciously at the unprotected arm. The sharp cutting brought a cry of rage and pain. Now the first boy staggered free. The one who'd drawn blood was too eager. At once he leaped in for a second jab, thinking the other was off balance. Too late he realised his mistake. Too late he saw the faint glint of light on moving metal as the blade sank into his side. With a deep sigh, he clamped a hand over the spurting wound falling back to the protection of the wall. This time the tables were reversed. It was the other one who now moved in for the kill.

'That's all,' ordered Benedict. 'I said that's all.'

As the kid made no move to obey, he brought the automatic down hard on the wrist holding the knife. The weapon clattered to the ground, and the boy screamed with pain.

'You better get him sewed up. That's a nasty cut you gave him.'

Benedict jerked the gun towards the silent figure by the wall. Both the late adversaries stood in shocked pain, staring hate at the madman with the gun. The first kid, the one who'd tried to run away, stirred suddenly and groaned.

'Hey, he's — you said he was dead,' muttered the one with the damaged wrist.

Benedict shook his head.

'No. You said that, not me. He'll be O.K. by tomorrow. Let me tell you punks something. One of the first things you have to learn in this world is to know the big-time when you see it. Remember that.'

Turning, he walked away. Toni staggered after him. She didn't want to go. She wanted to go to bed, or die, or throw up or something. Anything. What she didn't want was to go with Benedict.

He led her to the car, opened the rear door.

'Get in there,' he ordered. 'There's a towel on the seat. If you're not too shy, you can change your clothes too. There'll be something in that bag'll fit you. Don't worry about me. I'm not so old I have to get my kicks watching a bedraggled mess like you stripping off.'

Toni sat on the seat, staring straight ahead. She paid no attention to the towel and the travelling bag. Benedict ignored her as he swung into the driving seat, gunned the motor and rolled out into traffic.

The interior was warm and comfortable. Despite her feeling of unreality, Toni began gradually to relax. The blood and the pain of those kids was too recent to forget, but already the actuality of it all was becoming blurred, less sharp. Quite suddenly she shivered. Benedict flicked off the interior light.

'If you catch pneumonia I'll leave you out in the desert,' he promised. 'Now do like I told you. You're no use to me sick.'

She hesitated, then slowly her fingers moved towards one of the catches on the bag. Lifting back the lid, she tried to see what was inside.

'How'm I supposed to know what to wear when I can't see?' she grumbled.

Benedict gave a grunt and flicked the light back on. Toni looked at him, but he was staring out at the road ahead. One or two of the things in the bag didn't look half bad, she decided. She settled on a thick sweater and a dark green shirt. There was nothing to wear underneath, but the shivering reminded her she had no time to think about that.

'Taps,' she said.

Benedict doused the light. He hoped she hadn't been so long making up her mind that she would get sick. Not for her sake. As far as he was concerned, he didn't care what happened to her. But it would be an inconvenience to the operation, and that mattered. The big man had learned a long time ago that you had to expect things to go wrong when you set up a job. No matter how much thought and careful planning you put in, there was always something you forgot, or something you couldn't have foreseen. Sometimes it was circumstances, but more often it was people. Much more often it was people. And people getting sick at the wrong time was something nobody could guard against.

Behind him, Toni was struggling to free herself of the soaked red dress, which wrapped itself clammily round her shivering skin. Finally she made it, and after only a brief pause stripped off the black bra and pants. All the time she watched the big figure in the front seat, and never once did his eyes move from the road. Maybe he wasn't so bad after all. She got busy with the rough towel, grateful for the dry rasping against her body. In the confined space she found it a difficult and tiring job. She found her way into the heavy sweater, and revelled in the sudden glow of warmth as the soft wool slid over her shoulders. A few wriggles and she was into the skirt, snapping the clasp at her hip. The shivering was all gone now, replaced by this glow of well-being. Toni felt suddenly more relaxed, more like her usual self. Her hair must be a mess, she thought. There'd been a small vanity case inside the bag. Delving inside, she came up with a comb.

'Could we have some light again?' she asked.

The light went on, and she moved across the seat until she could see herself in the overhead driving mirror. As she began to comb her hair she found herself looking at the profile of Benedict. That was certainly a strong face, she admitted. Not bad-looking either, in a hard kind of way.

What was it he'd said back at Rugolo's? He could usually get it through the normal procedure. That wasn't hard to believe. Plenty of women could be drawn to this big muscular man with an air of getting his own way. She remembered the way he'd studiously avoided taking a peek while she was doing her fan-dance on the back seat. Well, she'd asked him not to look, and he hadn't. So why didn't he? How many men would have been able to resist just one or two sly glances? Not many. None in fact. So why didn't this Benedict, if that was really his name, which she doubted? Why shouldn't he look? What was wrong with her? Plenty of guys would have been glad of the chance. She had nothing to be ashamed of. A good figure, which stuck out where it was supposed to, without being meaty. Nice smooth skin. Why, most guys couldn't keep their hands off that velvet skin for five minutes. Who did Benedict think he was? Maybe he thought he was too good for her, she thought, in perverse fury.

'If you're through getting fixed, come and sit up front.'

His sudden voice, cutting into her thoughts, startled her.

'O.K.'

She gave her hair one final pat, and sat back. After a minute he said:

'Well? Are you ready?'

'Sure,' she agreed.

'Then what are you waiting for?' he demanded.

'Aren't you going to stop the car?' she queried.

'What for? Climb over the seat.'

She opened her mouth to say something, then checked it. She'd already found this was getting to be a habit around Benedict, and she'd do it a lot more before they were through. Setting her lips in an annoyed line, she clambered uncomfortably over, and down into the front seat. The green skirt rode up high on her legs, but the driver didn't seem to notice.

'You'll find a flask of brandy in the glove compartment,' he informed her. 'Drink some.'

'Brandy?' she replied. 'No thanks, I don't usually — '

'Do as I tell you,' he snapped. 'Don't want you to catch a chill or anything.'

She took out the flat flask and unscrewed the cup. Then, careful to avoid spilling any, she tipped out a measure of the dark amber fluid. Toni had never drunk brandy before, and she sniffed suspiciously at it.

'Drink it,' repeated Benedict.

Closing her eyes, she put the cup to her lips and tipped the contents down her

42

throat. Then she coughed, gasped, and two large tears formed in her eyes.

'O.K. Put it away.'

'Don't you — ?'

'Put it away. There's cigarettes and a lighter in there. Light one for me, too.'

She extracted two from the pack, snapped the lighter and bent her head over the flame. Then she handed one of the smokes to Benedict, who took it without a word and stuck it between his lips. She fondled the heavy gold lighter then put it back. Leaning back in the seat she inhaled deeply. Now that the shock of swallowing it was past, she could feel the comforting warmth of the brandy spreading out inside her. Maybe this wasn't going to be so bad, she reflected. At least it was a change from Rugolo's, and the place before Rugolo's, and the place before that. This was kind of an adventure almost. An adventure with shooting at the other end, she remembered with sudden cold. Quickly she shook the thought out of her mind. The cigarette was hitting the spot, and the spot was already warmed over with the brandy glow. He really was quite a man, this big guy sitting silently at her side. They had to stop sometime. They couldn't go on just driving for ever. And then, when they stopped, maybe it would be better. Maybe he'd loosen up a little bit. She'd like that, she knew. She'd like that a whole lot.

'Mr. Benedict,' she said quietly 'I'd like to ask something. Oh, it isn't about what we're doing or where we're going, or anything like that.'

'So?'

'It's about clothes. I mean, these are fine, these you loaned me. But I can't get through three or four days with just these.'

'We'll be in Steel City some time tomorrow. I'll advance you some dough, you get yourself fixed up.'

'Gee, thanks.'

'You'll pay it back out of your end,' he assured her evenly. 'We don't need the light any more.'

She switched it off and made a face in the new darkness. This was a cold-blooded fish, this Benedict. He hadn't needed to remind her about paying back the money, that had already been made clear at Rugolo's. Maybe he just liked pushing people around, let everybody know who's boss all the time.

Relaxed behind the wheel, Benedict thought about her. He didn't want to antagonise this broad, he remembered. What they were going to do called for teamwork, and nothing hits a team like personal squabbles. He'd better talk to her a while. Particularly as he didn't want her falling asleep.

I'll be asleep in a minute, thought Toni drowsily. The new comfort of the dry clothes, the brisk towelling and then the brandy, were all combining to make her realise how tired she was. She stretched back luxuriously and inhaled a lazy puff at the cigarette.

'Tell me about yourself,' Benedict said abruptly.

That brought her awake.

'Tell you what? I thought you knew all about me.'

'Only as much as I needed to know for my business. I don't know much outside of what I told you back there at the wop's.'

'Oh.'

She sat there, puzzled to know what he expected. It was the kind of question nobody asked her any more. Nobody, that is, who expected any other kind of answer than the kind they usually got.

'Um — um,' she faltered, 'not much to tell. My old man ran a drug store, it doesn't matter where. Any money he took in, he rushed into the nearest bar and got rid of it. My old lady gave up trying years ago. Soon as Rufe and me were old enough, we beat it.'

'Uh huh. And that's how you made out, him sticking up filling stations and such?'

'He did it for me,' she defended quickly. 'He's not a bad kid. Just wanted to get us a decent place, somewhere we could call a home, that's all.'

He wasn't really bad, not Rufe. Just sick and tired of being nobody and having nothing. It wasn't anybody else's fault but the old man's, but Rufe thought the whole world was to blame.

'And you?' queried Benedict. 'You could have taken up some other line of work, I imagine.'

Easy to talk. Specially when you're a man. Everything seems so easy for them.

'I tried working,' she told him. 'I worked in a store for forty-two fifty a week. The boss kept trying to lay me. When he saw I wasn't going to, he fired me. I was a car-hop for a time. That was worse. It wasn't only the boss there, it was two out of every three yaks who could afford to buy gas. I tried eight different jobs before I finally got wise. Everybody wanted one thing from me, and it had nothing to do with work. So I became a model. In two weeks I made better than six hundred dollars. Then the mob found out what I was doing. They wanted seventy-five per cent or they'd cut up my face. I blew town. That was who-knows how many towns ago. Now I'm here.'

'And the brother, Rufe, he's down there in San Antonio, praying for a big-league lawyer. Well, if we do all right, he'll get one.'

Yes, she thought, that's true. That's really true. This could be that big break everybody dreams about and never gets.

In the distance ahead she could make out a small sprinkling of lights.

'We coming to a town?'

'Nope. Motel,' he told her. 'We'll stop over for some sleep.'

That reminded her again of how tired she was. The idea of sleep had plenty of appeal. Five minutes later Benedict pulled the big sedan to a smooth stop in front of a lighted cabin. The broken neon tubing informed an uninterested world that this was the Desert Restova. Benedict slammed the door as he got out, then banged noisily on the cabin door. After a couple of minutes the door opened, and a man stood yawning in Benedict's face and scratching busily under an arm.

'Welcome folks, welcome,' he muttered. 'The Desert Restova — '

'Can that. Just give us a cabin,' interrupted Benedict.

The man stopped talking, looked at Benedict, and decided to agree with him.

'Number eleven,' he said. 'Straight down there, sixth one you come to on the left. You go on, I'll bring the key and fresh linen.'

Benedict climbed in beside Toni and eased off the brake. The car rolled slowly along the line of cabins, stopping at the sixth.

'Help me get this stuff out,' he snapped.

The proprietor, making his sleepy way towards them, saw Toni against the car lights. Fine looking woman, he thought. She reached inside the sedan and came out with a heavy bag. Well, one thing, they were sure married all right. Nobody who wasn't married to her would make a juicy woman like that lug the bags around. You get to learn a lot being in this business. If only these stray lovebirds knew how they give themselves away in a hundred different directions. Not like these two now. There, she'd dropped the bag.

'Be more careful, will you?'

Benedict's irritable voice carried clearly to the approaching man. Sure were married, right enough. Humping the sheets and towels under one arm, he walked up to the door and inserted the key. They all trooped inside. The room wasn't bad at all, Toni thought. Might have been a lot worse, stuck out in the middle of nowhere like this.

'Leave the stuff, we'll fix ourselves up.'

The man shrugged and dumped his burden on the bed. From a pocket he took a white card and a pen.

'If you'll just register Mr. — ?'

Mr. — ? left him standing there, and scribbled quickly on the card. Then he handed it back.

'Thank you Mr. Arnold. My name is Green. If there's anything — '

'Yeah. Good night.'

Green paused uncertainly.

'It being so late and all, Mr. Arnold, we usually like you to pay in advance after midnight.'

Without a word, Benedict took out his billfold and peeled off three fives.

'Will that take care of it?' he demanded.

'Oh yes, yes sir Mr. Arnold. That's fine. Maybe you and Mrs. Arnold would like a cup of coffee? No extra charge.'

Benedict was about to refuse when he saw the reaction on Toni's face. Well, where was the harm?

'O.K. Mr. Green, we'd like that. Thanks.'

Green was delighted to have done something which seemed to find favour with this big stranger. He went out at the run. Toni flashed a grateful smile at Benedict.

'Thanks,' she said. 'I know you did that for me. You don't want any coffee, do you?'

'I'll drink it when it comes. Get busy and fix this bed will you? I didn't stop here so we could chew the fat all night.'

She flushed, and began stripping off the covers. When Green came back five minutes later, Toni was sitting disconsolately at the side of the bed. Benedict was rinsing his hands at the washbasin.

'Here we are folks, all steaming hot,' announced the motel proprietor cheerfully. 'Hope this is the way you like it.'

He set down the wooden tray on a small table by the bed.

'That's fine,' grunted Benedict.

'Get you more sugar if you want,' offered Green.

'It's fine the way it is. Thanks. Good night.'

There was no conversational chink anywhere in the way the big stranger talked. Even the chatty Green knew he would be wasting his time if he tried to prolong the conversation. He grinned nervously and went out. Toni picked up one of the cups and sipped. The coffee was good. In the ordinary way she would never drink the stuff before going to bed, but tonight was unusual to say the least. And besides, the coffee was a way of filling in the time until Benedict gave her some idea of what was to happen next. A quick check in the bag had shown her there was nothing in there she could wear at night. Benedict finished patting at his face with the towel and threw it down.

'How's the coffee?' he demanded.

'Oh it's all right thanks. It's fine.'

He nodded, then crossed the room to stand looking down at her.

'You're scared of me, huh?'

She started to deny it, then shrugged.

'Yeah. I guess I am, a little.'

He grinned quickly. His teeth were too large to be perfect, but they were strong and white. Toni wished he'd smile more.

'That's good kid, that's good. It's good you should be afraid of me, because I am somebody to watch out for if people interfere with my plans. Don't ever do that, and you got nothing to be afraid of. Ketch?'

She nodded, unsure as to whether it would be all right to smile at the same time. She decided against it.

'And now you're wondering what the deal is here, right?'

She did smile slightly this time.

'Whatever deal you want, you get,' she replied simply. 'You're paying enough.'

Benedict shook his head quickly.

'I never paid a woman in my life,' he informed her curtly. 'What I hired you for, that's business. It don't include anything you don't want it to. Sleeping time is your own time. Whatever you do, it's your choice. You'll get no argument from me if you want to sleep by yourself, and you'll get no favours if you want it some other way.'

He began stripping off his shirt.

'When you finish your coffee, kill the light will you?'

He walked round to the other side of the bed and took off the rest of his clothes. The bed dipped suddenly behind Toni as his heavy weight settled on it. Then he stretched out and pulled the sheets over him. Toni sat cradling the cup in her hands and thinking over what Benedict had said. She didn't believe a word of it, but was puzzled as to why he should bother to tell her a yarn like that. Within ten minutes she'd know it wasn't true. Five, more likely. She set down the cup, walked over to the door and snapped off the light switch. Benedict or no Benedict, she wasn't going to try sleeping in the heavy sweater. Moonlight filtered its pale glow into the cabin as she pulled it over her head. Then she stepped free of the skirt and went to the bed. Pulling back the covers she slipped inside, staying as close to her own side as she could get. All the weariness returned as she lay back. It wouldn't be any use trying to sleep till afterwards, she knew that. Benedict lay silent, no more than a foot away. Why didn't he get on with it, she thought angrily. Gradually, the tension left her and she found herself sinking deeper into the mattress. Benedict neither spoke nor moved. Toni fought to keep her eyes open, but the lids kept dropping, and finally she felt herself drifting into sleep. She was past caring about anything.

4

A hand shook firmly at her shoulder. Immediately she came awake, events of the night flooding back into her consciousness. She shut her eyes again quickly at the brilliant sunshine streaming through the cabin windows. Benedict stood beside the bed, a cigarette dangling from his lips. He was fully dressed.

'Let's go,' he said 'Time to move.'

She nodded drowsily.

'What time is it?'

'Eleven thirty. When you sack out, you really go for it,' he told her.

'Do you mind?'

She pointed to where she'd dropped her clothes on the floor the previous night.

'Sure.'

He went to a window, and stood staring out. Quickly she dived out of bed and put on her things. The sweater weighed a ton in the hot, dry atmosphere. She went to the case and took out a linen shirt. Benedict had not moved. Yanking the sweater off she slipped into the shirt, glad of the smooth coolness against her skin.

'O.K.,' she announced.

He turned around and looked at her appraisingly. She wondered again what kind of man he was, thinking back to the night. It wasn't that he didn't go for women, she was sure of that. It also wasn't that there was anything wrong with what she was carrying around. She knew better than that.

'Have I got time to wash up?' she demanded.

Benedict nodded.

'I'll go wait in the car. Be out in five minutes.'

He went out, shutting the door behind him. Some day, she thought with quick anger, I'm going to get some kind of emotion out of you. But she only had five minutes, and couldn't waste time with her thoughts.

Benedict sat in the driver's seat smoking steadily, and busy with his thoughts. The girl was going to be O.K.

he reflected. Mob girls were all right in their place, and their place was in a horizontal position. They were no use for what he wanted done. Cops could spot a mob girl on sight, and once spotted they might as well be dead. This girl handled herself with a kind of assurance, which was a mile removed from the brash swagger of those others. Yes, so far so good.

With seconds of the five minutes remaining, Toni came out of the cabin lugging the bag. Benedict checked his watch, and noted with satisfaction that she'd obeyed him literally. That was good, too. That was the kind of thinking they were going to need if they were ever to pull off the caper.

Toni opened the rear door, and heaved the bag on to the seat. Then she climbed in beside Benedict and said:

'Do we ever get to eat on this job?'

'There's a diner about forty miles along. Thought we'd make it there before we ate.'

She settled back, noting the smooth way he handled the car, backing away from the cabin and swinging out into a wide arc onto the road.

'You'll find some dark glasses in the compartment at the back,' he told her. 'Get them out, will you?'

She did as he asked, passing one pair to him. Then she put on the smaller pair, glad of the immediate relief from the glare of the concrete strip and the baked sand either side of it. They passed only one other vehicle, a truck, on the journey to the diner. Benedict kept the pedal close to the floor the whole way, and they passed a wooden hoarding thirty minutes after leaving the motel. The notice announced that The Waterhole was open twenty-four hours a day.

It wasn't much of a place, thought Toni, as they braked in the almost deserted parking lot. The smell of the food inside caused her to revise her opinions. Until that moment she'd been thinking she was no more than averagely hungry. They sat by a window, Benedict selecting a chair from which he could watch the road. She noted the way his eyes moved frequently to the highway.

Surely he wasn't expecting anybody to be following them, she wondered? Not that she would dare to ask anyway. The arrival of the food soon pushed all speculation from her mind. She attacked it with real enthusiasm, and found it was good. Benedict ate sparingly, with deft neat movements, and seemed to be not very hungry. He finished long before the girl and sat nursing a glass of cold beer and watching her unobtrusively. He was wondering what she had made of his attitude the previous night. Remembering the way the moonlight had played on her body, and looking at her now, he realised he could scarcely blame her if she thought he was a fairy. As the thought came into his mind, the corners of his mouth pulled quickly into the faint hint of a smile.

'What is it, am I eating too much?' demanded the girl.

'Eat all you want,' he replied. 'I'm not thinking about you at all.'

'I'm about through anyway,' she told him.

They sat awhile over cigarettes, not talking. Finally, it was close to one p.m.

when Benedict paid the check and they left. Back on the road she spoke again.

'You said something about me buying clothes in Steel City,' she reminded. 'That sign said Steel is one hundred and ten miles from here. The stores stay open all night there?'

'We'll be there,' he grunted.

The indicator on the clock crept slowly upwards. Toni didn't like speed, and wished she hadn't asked the question. The needle flickered on to the 90 and stayed there. Mile after mile flashed by, the unbroken flatness of the desert seeming so lifeless as to be unreal. It was hot in the car, and Toni began to understand why Benedict had hardly eaten anything. She felt the heaviness of her eyes, and the unshakeable drowsiness stealing over her. If she'd been driving at that speed, they would have wound up in a smoking heap at the side of the road. Again she felt that grudging admiration for the big man beside her. He thought of everything, in advance. It all helped to give her confidence in the outcome of whatever it was they were going to do.

Yes, she thought sleepily, this Benedict was some operator —

'Wake up.'

The harsh voice at her ear brought her upright with a start.

'I wasn't asleep — ' she began to protest.

'You would have been in another ten seconds,' he grated. 'Talk about something.'

'Well — what?'

'Something — anything — it doesn't matter. Just talk. You like the movies?'

It was an unusual time for the question. Toni stared at him.

'Yeah, I guess so.'

'So talk about the movies. When did you go last?'

She began to talk. Normally, she liked to talk, but this was different. It was unnerving, somehow, trying to make conversation to instructions. Haltingly, she began telling him about her most recent visit to the movies. He asked questions, and gradually she began to speak more easily.

Benedict didn't take his eyes off the

road. Beside him, the girl prattled on, an endless fountain of words which he hardly heard at all. He wasn't having anybody dropping off to sleep when he wasn't asleep, not when they were working for him. It seemed harmless enough, letting people sleep. But you let them do that, let them get ahead with their sleeping time, and the next thing he knew they'd be awake when he was asleep. And that would be bad, that's always bad. In an operation like this, there could only be one wheel, one top man. And the top man had to know what everybody else was doing, all the time. If he didn't know their every move, he couldn't control them, and once he lost control of their movements, their contacts, he would no longer be entirely certain of the odds against him. He suddenly put his hand to his inside jacket pocket and took out his wallet.

'Here.'

Toni was in mid-sentence when the brown pigskin was thrust at her. Wonderingly she took it.

'What's this?'

'Take out two hundred bucks and give it back,' he ordered.

She opened it slowly and stared at the folded money inside. Nervously she extracted a bill.

'That's a hundred,' he snapped. 'That's no good. Take tens and twenties.'

She nodded, and put the hundred back. Then she counted out other bills carefully.

'Two hundred,' she said. 'You want to count it?'

By way of reply he stuck out his hand for the wallet. Then, without looking at it, he shoved it back inside his coat. The girl pushed the bills into a neat pile. When Benedict had said he'd stake her to a few clothes she hadn't expected anything like this.

'I don't really need this much, you know,' she told him.

'You need it,' he assured her. 'You're not going to buy junk. You're going to buy just enough things to see you through a couple or three days. Good things, like class. You come back with junk and I'll burn it. Then I'll make you go again with

64

another lot of money, and it all comes out of your end, see? So it's your own dough you'll be fooling with, not mine.'

'I get it,' she said, half to herself. 'The duds go with what we're going to do.'

'Just do as I tell you,' Benedict replied. 'No junk.'

At two thirty they passed the first building they'd seen since the diner. This was a ramshackle chicken farm that lay back off the road. Benedict dropped his speed to sixty, and soon they were passing more and more evidence of civilisation. Little groups of houses, a filling station. There was light traffic now, and all the signs of the outskirts of a busy small town. She noticed the way Benedict drove into the town. Careful, smooth driving, always giving the other guy the benefit of the doubt, avoiding all risks. Most of the people she'd known who thought they were big shots were always acting big time. Pushing people around, shouting at waiters, crowding others off the roads as they swung their big jazzy cars around. They always had the best, they made sure everybody knew it. And yet somehow you knew they weren't the best. They were loud and aggressive, always out there in front, but you knew they weren't the best. Benedict wasn't like that. His clothes were good, but they didn't carry a neon sign advertising the fact. His car was one of the best, but it wasn't pink and yellow. He didn't toss his weight around, but people seemed to know the weight was there. Look at the way he handled Rugolo. Most people payed attention when Rugolo was talking, but this big quiet man talked to him as though he were a lackey. And Rugolo acted like one, too. This driving into Steel City, this was something to learn from. Many times Benedict could have used his size and extra speed to beat another driver to a traffic space, but he never bothered. Toni was secretly pleased with herself for knowing why. There'd be no tickets for Benedict, no need for any traffic policeman to recall the car or the occupants. She remembered something another man had told her long before. If you want to break some big laws, don't use up any strength breaking a lot of little ones.

They were into the city now, and she looked around with interest. She'd seen a lot of towns, and they all came to the same thing in the end, that much she knew. But she hadn't yet lost the traveller's hope that this place would somehow be better than the last. Benedict swung into a parking space in the shopping centre, and pointed out of the window.

'That's the best store for what you want. Martin's.'

She looked at the eight-storey building and nodded.

'O.K. Where'll I see you?'

'I'll be behind you,' he replied. 'You may need a nickel for a 'phone call.'

'Listen,' she began. 'Don't you trust me yet? Why would I want to call anybody?'

'Who knows?' he shrugged. 'People do funny things. I won't bother you. Just get good stuff.'

She pursed her lips and nodded. They climbed out and went into Martin's. For the next two hours she enjoyed herself. Really enjoyed herself, in a way she hadn't done for a long time. Benedict was around, but he was as good as his word and never interfered. Once, she had her hands on a cheap shiny blouse. There was no intention of buying it, she was merely interested, but in the glass behind the sales counter she saw that Benedict was watching. She put it down quickly and moved on to something else, and after that didn't even look at anything of the kind. Toni had no inkling of the way time was slipping by. She was just an ordinary woman now, out on a big spend, and time had no relevance. Finally, as she accepted change from the latest purchase, she realised with mild surprise that she had exactly fourteen fifty left of the two hundred dollars. That, and an unmanageable heap of wrapped purchases. She began to pile all the bags together, and could see she wasn't going to be able to carry everything at once. A man walked up to her.

'Excuse me, ma'am, but you seem to have bought half the store. I'm the floor manager. May I help you with all this down to your car?'

She looked quickly for Benedict, but he

was nowhere on view. To refuse the offer, she decided, would be unwise and could attract attention. She treated the dapper man before her to one of her flashing smiles.

'Why, you're very kind,' she trilled. 'My husband seems to have disappeared. He can't stand it when I'm shopping.'

The manager smiled pleasantly. It was his practice, not to say his stock in trade, to smile at the customers. But with this one it came naturally. There are some women men will always smile at, and Toni Graham was one of them. Now she loaded up the manager with bags and parcels the way any woman would have done. She took her time about it, so that if Benedict objected he'd have plenty of time to show up and make like an overdue husband. When the manager was almost hidden from view, she scooped up the remaining bags and swept out of the place, the heaped-up man behind her a bad second. Out on the street she pointed across to the car.

'We're parked over there,' she announced.

'That is, if it isn't too much trouble?'

'A pleasure, ma'am, for a customer like yourself,' a voice assured her from the paper and plastic heap.

As they neared the car she saw Benedict. He was leaning against a convertible further down the parking line, and reading a newspaper. Slowly he shook his head.

'We'll have to dump it all on the ground if he's locked it,' she complained. But the door opened at a touch, and the manager was able to unload. Toni made a fuss of him, gave him another smile that made his heart beat a little faster for the rest of that day, then got rid of him. She climbed into the car and waited.

Minutes ticked away and Benedict made no attempt to move from the convertible. Finally he straightened, tossed the paper in a nearby trash-can, came back to the car and got in.

'Say, I'm sorry about that guy,' she began quickly. 'It would've looked bad if I refused.'

Benedict turned the cold eyes towards

her, and again she wished she could learn to read the signs in that stare.

'You did the right thing,' he replied, in brief measured tones. 'It's company policy at Martin's to help people carry their stuff if they spend more than a hundred dollars in the store. And it looks like you did.'

He looked quickly at the untidy heap of loot.

'I spent a hundred and eighty-six dollars,' she told him. 'You want the change?'

'Uh uh,' he negatived.

He waited for a break in the traffic then moved the car into it.

'We'll get a cup of coffee, then I have to see a couple of people. You wait in the car.'

They found a small lunch counter, and had coffee and sandwiches. Benedict didn't talk to her and they had the food in silence.

'Let's go, if you're all through,' he clipped.

She went out with him, and he drove into the shabby end of town, braking outside a barber shop.

'I won't be long. Stay right here.'

She watched him go inside, wondering idly what he'd want with a barber. The place didn't look much, kind of run-down to her way of thinking. Not that she had a lot of time for thinking because Benedict re-appeared, a little man showing him out with every sign of friendliness. She was amazed to see Benedict smile broadly and clap the little man on the shoulder. So the guy was part-human at least.

There was no sign of the smile when he got back in the car. After a few minutes driving he stopped again.

'Last call. You stay put.'

Stay put, stay here, don't move. Where the hell did he think she was going? There wasn't anybody in town she knew, and even if there was someone she might like to know she wasn't likely to find him in this crummy section. Benedict was longer this time, and nobody showed him out of the building when he came, so there was no second showing of the smile. Now he drove off in silence, and she was glad to notice an improvement in the streets they now passed through. It was obvious Benedict knew the lay-out of Steel City very well and knew exactly where he was making for, which turned out to be a reasonable looking small hotel called the Hotel York. She sat quietly, waiting to be told what to do.

'Shove that stuff in your bag,' he said.

Reaching over into the rear, he hauled the bag over and gave it to her. She tried to open it and do as she was told, but there wasn't enough room.

'Okay, I'll get out.'

He stepped out on to the sidewalk and stretched. Quickly, she put all the things she'd bought inside and closed the lid with difficulty. He leaned in, grabbed the bag and put it down outside. She clambered out.

'Now what?' she demanded.

'Now we go in,' he told her.

Turning, he walked towards the door of the hotel. Toni shrugged, picked up the bag and followed him. He went to the desk and booked a double room for the night. Toni stood wondering why they hadn't made for the next town which was only eighty miles further on. With a tingle of quiet excitement she wondered whether this might be the end of the line, Steel City. This could be the place where they were going to do it, whatever it was. Benedict signed the register, took a key from the old man behind the desk.

'Wait here.'

She stood and waited while he went back out to the car. The old man watched her, wondering why the good-looking ones always fell for these big apes who didn't know how to treat a woman. Benedict came back, carrying a bag of his own which looked heavy. Without a word he walked past her to the stairs, and she followed him up in silence. At the second floor he found the room, pushed the key in the lock and they went in.

It wasn't a bad room, thought Toni. Certainly she'd seen a lot worse. Benedict shut the door, locked it and put the key in his pocket.

'This is it for a few hours,' he said in a flat tone. 'You'll be like a cat with fleas till you've tried on all that stuff a dozen times. Now's your chance.'

74

She wondered quickly whether he was one of those creepy ones, who got their kicks watching women dress and undress. In a room this size she certainly wasn't going to get any privacy. Benedict took off his coat and threw it on a chair. The wallet and gun he stuck under a pillow, then he stretched out on the big bed.

'We'll be driving all night,' he informed her. 'You'll be able to sleep in the car, but not me. So I'm getting mine now. You do what you want till ten o'clock. O.K.?'

Without waiting for an answer, he turned his back to her and settled down to sleep. She hesitated, then put the bag on a chair, unfastened the catches and lifted out the first Martin's wrapping. It seemed all wrong, she reflected. What was it this guy needed that she hadn't got? Last night O.K. Maybe last night he'd been bushed, but not this time. He had a good sleep behind him, and all he'd done was a few hours driving. This time it was like a calculated insult, going to sleep like that as though she wasn't there. She peeked in the bag. It was the lumberjack shirt, the one with the patch pockets. That ought to go good with those tan jeans she'd bought. Or maybe it would look better with the — . Off now in a private world exclusive to women, she began to take off her clothes.

★ ★ ★

She woke with a start, to find the room in darkness. The deep chair, in which she'd fallen asleep after a glorious hour of clothes switching, had given her a crick in the neck. What time was it? Crossing to the window, she looked out into the street. A brightly-lit clock-face told it was ten after ten. Benedict seemed to be still asleep, and she didn't know how to set about waking him up. If she touched him there was no telling what he might do. Maybe hit her, or come up fast with the gun, thinking somebody was trying to jump him. Of course, the lights, Toni found the switch and snapped it down.

Benedict stirred at once, came awake completely.

'Ten minutes after ten,' she advised him. 'You said we'd be moving out.'

'Yeah.'

He rubbed a hand quickly over his face, then looked round at her.

'Thought you'd be wearing some of the new duds.'

'Not to stretch out in a car,' she replied firmly.

The ghost of a smile flickered in his eyes.

'O.K. Pack up. We got places to go.'

5

The noisy jangle of a cheap alarm clock brought a weary groan from the figure on the bed. An arm was flung out to end the torture, and for a full minute there was silence again in the room. Then the figure wriggled, cursed, sat upright and became a man in his early twenties. Not a young man, merely a man in his early twenties. Tip Brennan had evolved from gutter urchin into man shortly after the age of thirteen. He'd been the youngest of a gang who broke into a cigar store in the small hours of the morning. The store owner, an old man, heard the noise and came to investigate. The older boys were uncertain what to do about him, but Tip showed no hesitation. He grabbed a metal lever, used for opening packing crates, and hit the old man across the base of the skull. He then gave curt orders to the others to get on with the steal, and they did what he said. The owner of the store was lucky. After two weeks in hospital he was as good as new, and he couldn't identify any of his attackers. The boys got clean away, and Tip learned a valuable lesson. Since that night he had repeated it to himself in private a thousand times. You got to do it to the other guy first. He had been doing it fairly regularly ever since.

Now he scratched under his chin and checked the time by the elegant gold-plated strapwatch on his hairy arm. It was seven-thirty in the evening. He already knew that from the alarm bell, but it gave him more pleasure to look at the watch. It was his own property, honestly paid for, and he had a receipt to prove it. As he never tired of explaining, everything about you has to be legit. Anybody who keeps stolen property for his own use is a sucker. You get something that's hot, you get rid of it. Then you use the money to buy things from stores, like everybody else does. And always get a receipt. If the cops catch you with just one piece of hot merchandise they might be able to nail you for six, ten, twenty other jobs you were mixed up in. Because cops are smart. Cops have system, they got organisation, crime labs like on the T.V. programmes. Cops are smart all right, and anybody don't think so is just a big mouth on his way to stir.

In the midst of these reflections Tip became aware that someone had banged on the door. Annoyed, he shouted:

'Who is it?'

'Message from Mr. Prescott,' replied a voice, a man's.

Immediately Tip sprang from the bed and stood to one side of the door. Sliding open a noiseless drawer, he felt his fingers curl round the smooth metal inside.

'C'mon in,' he shouted. 'It ain't locked.'

The handle turned and a man walked in, looking towards the bed. Tip pushed at the door with his foot and it slammed shut. The man turned quickly, to find himself staring at a short-nosed .45 revolver. Tip noted at once that there was no trace of fear in the calm eyes.

'What's that for?' asked the visitor dispassionately.

Tip was sizing him up, and the more he saw, the more he congratulated himself on his foresight in grabbing the gun.

'What it's for is to shoot people,' he replied easily. 'I squeeze this little thing my finger's resting on. A hunk of lead flies out of that hole you're looking at, and you're all through looking.'

The man chuckled, which wasn't the expected reaction.

'And why do you want to shoot me?'

'I don't know yet. Maybe I won't have to. One thing though, you don't have any message from Charlie. Go sit on the bed.'

The big man shrugged, walked across and perched on the rumpled bed. Tip watched him narrowly.

'Charlie don't send no messages,' he informed the other nastily. 'Or if he does he don't send strangers. Who are you and what do you want?'

'Prescott told me I might be able to use you, but I don't know,' he replied.

'Use me?' Tip didn't need to pretend surprise. 'You use me? That's a good one. Nobody tells me what to do but Charlie Prescott.'

The man nodded.

'I know. And who do you imagine tells him?'

This was too much for Brennan, too much thinking. This was Steel City. Charlie Prescott ran the town. You worked for Charlie you worked for the top man. So who could tell Charlie? This guy was crazy. No. This guy wasn't crazy. The way he wore clothes, the way he carried himself, Tip had seen those signs before. The way this feller walked in, like he owned the pad, the way he thumbed his nose at the heater.

'I asked you a question,' the visitor reminded him.

'I know it. Wait a minute, I'm thinking.'

The man on the bed noted with approval that the gun didn't waver. This kid might be worried and uncertain, but he wasn't losing sight of the essentials.

Tip was remembering the last time he'd seen two guys like this one. They'd called on Charlie at the barber shop one day. He'd taken them in a back room, sent somebody out for champagne, at ten o'clock in the morning. The two spoke to

Charlie the way nobody in Steel City would dare. Almost like he was the guy who ran the messages or something. After they went Charlie was very quiet. Then next day, somebody put a bomb in Greek Eddie's car and that was the end of Eddie. Charlie never talked about it, and Tip knew better than to ask questions. Now here was another guy, an operator like those two the other time. And he wanted Tip. This could be the big break, the one Charlie told him about. But he didn't know yet.

'You say you been talking to Charlie,' he demanded suspiciously, 'How do I know that?'

'Call him,' was the bored reply.

'Don't think I won't.'

He shoved the gun in his pocket, felt for change, and went out to the pay-phone in the hall. He was connected almost at once.

'Mr. Prescott? Say, this is Tip. Got a man here, says he's a friend of yours.'

Charlie's quiet careful voice spoke at the other end.

'So why call me?'

'Gee, Mr. Prescott, I never saw this guy before,' Tip protested. 'He could be here to make trouble for all I know.'

Charlie tutted with disgust.

'For all you know,' he mimicked. 'All you know is nothing. Just nothing, you hear? That man is an important business contact of mine. When he talks you jump, boy, or you'll regret it. I don't know what he wants and I ain't asking. Just do like he tells you and you might learn something. And keep your mouth shut, or you might get it fixed that way.'

The loud noise in his ear told Tip the receiver had been slammed down. Thoughtfully he hung up and went back to his room. The visitor was sitting where he'd left him.

'Well, did you talk to Prescott?' he demanded.

'Yeah,' admitted Tip. 'I talked with him. He says O.K.'

'So O.K., let's get down to cases.'

Tip nodded, pulled over a chair and sat near the big man.

'You talk, mister. I'm listening.'

'That's the first thing, and you got it

right. It's a good sign. When I talk, you listen.'

The cold eyes bored into his face and Tip nodded slowly. Deep down, he knew this was the big one. All the years of dirty work, petty thieving, beatings, that was the build-up. A guy had to learn the business so he'd be ready when it happened. It was going to happen now. He felt the stir of excitement inside him, but was careful to reveal nothing on his face.

'I'm running a little thing, and I can use somebody like you,' the other continued. 'You should be back here inside four days, but I can't guarantee it. There are angles to the caper, all kinds of angles. If I don't like the way anything's going, any small part of it, the whole thing is off. I don't take chances. Guys who take chances give me a sore belly. So you may get to do nothing at all. If that's the way it drops, I'll pay a grand for your time.'

A grand. Tip moistened his lips with a dry tongue. If he didn't do anything, he collected a thousand dollars. This had to be some operation. The other man smiled inside as he saw the quick movement of Tips tongue, the only outward sign of emotion on the otherwise impassive face.

'Now I'll tell you what happens if we do the thing.' He paused significantly. 'Your end will be twenty thousand dollars.'

The stirring excitement inside Tip erupted now into a wild surge. He jumped up from the chair and prowled around the room. Finally he stopped, half-grinned at his visitor.

'Say,' he breathed. 'Say.'

The man nodded.

'That's the figure. For that, you do what I tell you, when I tell you. Prescott tells me you know how to take orders. You'll need to, because once you're in, you're in. The way out is feet first. Kabish?'

'Got it.'

Tip was scarcely listening. His mind was a mad turmoil of thoughts, all starting out from a big green figure that said twenty thousand. With that a man could do anything, be anything. For that, a man would do anything. What was this crazy guy talking about, people walking away from that kind of dough? He didn't know Tip Brennan, if he imagined Tip would take any chances on lousing up a deal like that.

'When do we start?' he queried.

'Not so fast,' cautioned the other. 'We get to ask a few questions first.'

Questions yet. Who needed questions? Let's just get out there and get on with the thing, man. The twenty thousand thing. Now the man was asking him something.

'Drink?' repeated Tip. 'No. Never touch it. It don't bring nothing but trouble, and it makes a guy look like a pig.'

'How about dope?' was the next question.

Tip laughed with scorn.

'Do I look like a junkie?' he demanded. 'Go ahead, search the joint. Here.'

He pulled up his shirt sleeve, revealing the bunched muscle of his upper arm. The man nodded.

'Keep your temper,' he warned. 'At these prices, you shouldn't get excited over a few simple questions. There's something else, something that can cause just as much trouble as booze and junk. And that's women.'

There was a heavy pause. Tip wasn't able to laugh quite so readily as with the other questions. Hesitantly he said:

'Look, mister, I don't know what you want me to say. I ain't no fairy. When I want a woman I take one. There isn't nobody special, if that's what you mean.'

'That's a start,' was the reply. 'But it doesn't go far enough. There are plenty of guys in this world who can't stay away from women, even for a few days.'

'Is that all?' Tip sighed with relief. 'Listen, I could do without one for months if I had to. And for that kind of money I'd have to. I won't go near one till you say.'

He was buoyant again. There'd been times in the past when he'd gone without women, for the simple reason he couldn't afford it. So you just stayed away from them. Easy. But the man was shaking his head.

'It's not as simple as that. There's a

woman in this. You'll be close to her for days, hardly out of her sight. She's the one you stay away from. Now you get the point?'

Was that all? This guy had some broad with him, and he didn't want anybody muscling in. He needn't worry about that. No lousy dame was going to make Tip Brennan risk twenty grand. For that he could have almost any dame in the whole world.

'It's O.K., mister, don't worry about it. I'm used to having dames around and I can handle it.'

His hesitation had been noted with satisfaction. If he had immediately protested, he would have talked himself out of the deal, and twenty thousand dollars would have walked out the door. But he had paused, thought it over and then replied. It would do.

'Then that's about all from me. Your turn to ask questions.'

Again Tip waited before speaking. Questions were something he'd learned to dispense with years earlier. People don't like to be asked questions. If they wanted you to know something, they told you. If they didn't tell you, you didn't poke your nose in. It was as simple as that. Still, a deal like this was unusual. There was one question that had been nagging away in his mind ever since the big stranger first told him the proposition.

'Er, don't get sore,' he mumbled. 'But you did say O.K. for questions. This deal, there'll be some heavy work?'

Rape, assault, robbery, these were Tip's normal stock in trade. There were very few illegal acts he hadn't committed at one time or another. But the heavy work, the final act of taking the life of a fellow human being, this was something he'd never done. It wasn't that he shrank from the idea. He'd thought about it many times, wondered what he'd do when he finally had to face it. This could be the time. The big man stared at him coldly.

'Why? Does it bother you?'

'No,' he replied, too quickly. 'No, I just want to know where I stand, that is all.'

'There could be,' he was told tersely. 'You want out?'

'No.'

There was no hesitation in the denial. He did not want out. He wanted to get his hands on that money, and if somebody had to die in the process, that was tough luck for them. The other seemed satisfied.

'Anything else you want to know?' he demanded.

'Just one. If we're gonna be together four days, what do I call you?'

To his surprise the visitor got up from the bed.

'Don't go out,' he warned. 'Don't talk to anybody. Stay away from the phone. Throw together whatever you'll need while you're away. Somebody's watching you. If you do as you're told, I'll be back just before midnight. Then we go. If you don't do what I told you, you'll never see me again. And I'll leave word with Prescott you're unreliable.'

The last sentence chilled Brennan. To be marked unreliable would be the end of his career with the quiet barber.

'I'll be here,' he promised. 'Oh, say, I'll need cigarettes.'

The man reached in his pocket, and a

shiny pack flopped quietly on the bed.

'Thanks.'

Then the other was gone. Tip stared at the closed door for a whole minute, before crossing to the bed and picking up the cellophane-wrapped pack.

'King Jack,' he muttered. 'The best. Nothing but the best.'

Stretching out on the bed, he carefully stripped off the wrapping and selected a fat cigarette. The big man, the operator, had said he was being watched. The big guy might be smart, but he wasn't a swami. An idea occurred to him, and he swung his legs down off the bed, and sat up. The only way anybody could see inside the room was through the window.

Crossing to it, he raised it up and leaned out. The dying light of the sun was still strong enough for him to see clearly into the street below. Down there was nothing unusual, nothing he hadn't seen on a hundred other nights. Puzzled, he stared down again, and then suddenly he knew. Very slowly he raised his head and stared, not down, but straight across at the building opposite. Seated in a window, a man waved cheerily and nodded. So that was it.

He nodded curtly in reply, then moved around picking up the few things he'd need for the trip, and shoving them in a small grip that he dragged from under a nest of drawers. It was almost nine o'clock. If the big man was coming at twelve he might as well sack out for a while. For all he knew he might need to be up all night. Reaching for the light, he was about to flip it off when he checked himself. If he put off the light, the guy across the street wouldn't be able to see into the room. And if he couldn't see in, he couldn't report with certainty on Tip's activities. Leave the light alone. But if he was on the bed, the watcher still couldn't see him. Making up his mind, he grabbed at the bed and heaved it across in front of the window. Then he made a dumb show to indicate he was going to sleep. The man in the building opposite waved again, to show he understood. Tip nodded, pleased with his own ingenuity, then rolled on the bed and was quickly asleep.

Something woke him. It was quite dark outside now, and he checked quickly at his strap-watch. It was five minutes short of midnight. Better get ready for his visitor. As he heaved himself sideways he started suddenly. Sitting in a chair facing him was the man he'd been waiting for.

'I didn't hear you come in,' said Tip lamely.

'People don't, usually,' acknowledged the other. 'You did all right, you used your head. You still want in?'

'Natch.'

'Then it's settled. Call me Benedict.'

The name sent a warm glow into Tip's mind. Of itself, it meant nothing. He'd never heard it before, and chances were it wasn't even the guy's regular name. But it was a name, and that meant it was real. No more just around the corner, but now.

'Glad to know you Mr. Benedict.'

'We'll just get a few things straight, then we'll get going. First, don't ever be in doubt about who's running things. That's me, and I don't want any arguments. When I tell you to do something you jump. This is not some penny-ante operation like roughing up some poor guy in a delicatessen for a lousy ten-dollar due. It's big, and when you have something big it has to be controlled every inch of the way. Somebody has to do that job, and that somebody is me.'

'Sure, Mr. Benedict. You're the boss, no doubt about it.'

'Don't have any doubts about it, and we'll get along. The woman is outside. I don't want you getting cosy. No talk about the job we're doing, no talk about yourselves. You wanta talk, talk about the weather, the movies, any damned thing. But impersonal. Yes?'

'Yessir. I got it.'

'All right. Your stuff ready'

'Sure.'

He grabbed the small bag and stood waiting. Benedict looked at him.

'You got a heater in there?'

'Sure thing,' he nodded. 'You said — '

'Get rid of it,' snapped the big man. 'I don't want anything like that around. The law can trace guns faster than a flea.'

'Oh, you don't have to worry about this

one,' Tip began. 'The numbers — '

His voice tailed away at the steely glint in Benedict's eyes. Snapping open the catches on the grip he took out the gun and tossed it in a drawer. Benedict nodded.

'Let's go.'

At the door he turned. Tip, immediately behind, almost cannoned into him.

'Don't tell the woman where we're going,' snapped the big man.

'How could I? I don't know where we're going,' Tip replied in surprise.

'Oh, didn't I tell you? You asked earlier about heavy work. I thought we'd get that little problem out of the way at the start. You're going to kill somebody.'

6

They walked downstairs in silence. Tip
Brennan's mind was in a turmoil again,
but not this time with wild dreams of
the promised land. Those flowed from a
later period, days from now, when he'd
have twenty thousand greenbacks in his
pocket. Ten minutes ago, those few days
had figured as a brief interlude in time, an
unknown area with maybe a dark corner
or two that he'd look into if and when the
time came. A few days after all, is only a
few days. Correction, was only a few days.
Now they seemed to stretch menacingly
into the far future, an endless period of
uncertain dangers and hidden pitfalls.
The dark corners were no longer remote
and scattered, they were all around.
You're going to kill a man. That's what
Benedict had said, just like that. Anybody
would've thought he was saying, what
time is the train? or what'll you drink?
Only he wasn't saying that at all. He was

saying, you're going to kill a man, and he meant it. Already there was sweat on Tip's forehead, a cold layer of dampness that had nothing to do with the temperature of the air. This was a sweat of fear and apprehension, and he knew that his throat was dry too and under the thin jacket his heart was pumping at a furious pace.

Ahead of him, Benedict walked unhurriedly. He knew what was going on in Tip's mind and he had intended the reaction he was getting. If this old-young man was going to be relied on in the coming work, it was no use waiting until the job was in process before learning whether or not the reliance was justified. That could get all kinds of people killed and also, more important, jeopardise the caper. Brennan seemed to meet every requirement except this one important detail of whether or not he would kill. Tonight they would find out.

Down on the street, a big sedan waited silently at the kerb. Another time, Tip would have noted all its finer points with appreciation. Now, in the darkness of the street, it only made him think of a hearse.

'In the front,' clipped Benedict. 'I drive.'

Tip climbed in and the door swung to with the softest of clicks. He hunched miserably, staring out at the familiar street. Familiar, yet somehow a thing of which he was no longer a part. He was cut off from that life by an automobile door and a silent figure who sat beside him, bringing the motor to smooth efficient life. There was perfume in the interior and his nose wrinkled appreciatively at the familiar smell. Must be the big guy's dame, the one he had to keep his hands off. Not that this was any time to be thinking about dames. This was a time for worrying about what was to happen when the car reached its destination, and the chill words were translated into grim reality. It was as easy as that, he reflected. When the car stopped, he was supposed to kill somebody. Not next week, not some time when the chips were down, but right here, now, tonight. And he didn't even know who it was going to be.

Benedict drove with his usual smooth

perfection, saying nothing. Now and then he glanced quickly at the overhead mirror to get a glimpse of the tense face of the man beside him. They were almost at their destination now, and in about ten minutes Tip Brennan would have taken the irrevocable step that placed him squarely in the major league. He made a left turn and brought the car to a stop outside a tall office building.

'Out.'

He nudged Brennan with his elbow. Like a man in a dream, Tip released the catch on his door and stepped out on to the street.

Benedict turned and said, 'We'll be back in ten minutes.'

From the rear of the car a voice, a woman's, replied, 'O.K.'

Tip heard her with surprise and tried to peer into the rear seat as he closed the door. He hadn't registered there was someone else in the car, and it didn't make him feel any better. The woman was only one more potential witness against him for the future. Benedict had already walked into a narrow opening at the side of the building and Tip had to walk fast to catch him. He was puzzled to know what they were doing here at the very end of the Steel City business section. There wouldn't be anybody down here to kill except maybe a night watchman. Maybe that was it, maybe they were going to rob some warehouse or something. No. Benedict had said ten minutes, and you don't rob a warehouse in that time. The big man moved confidently from one alleyway to another. Tip knew the town well, and it was evident his new boss did, too. They walked for about three minutes, then Benedict stopped suddenly. They were standing by an old warehouse, badly in need of a paint job. To the right a narrow cutting ran for fifty yards to what Tip knew to be Oasis Street, the town's Skid Row. Here were the cheap bars, the gambling joints, the brothels. The Street catered to the bum trade, and it was said you got the cheapest, and by definition the worst, of everything on Oasis Street. Benedict looked at his watch.

'Within the next four minutes,' he whispered, 'A man will turn round that corner and head this way. He's the one.'

Tip's heart leaped, but he tried to keep emotion off his face as he nodded.

'What do I use, my hands?'

To his relief, his voice sounded quite normal and controlled. By way of an answer, Benedict took something from his pocket. It was an old-fashioned revolver, polished a bright silver. Like some damned cowboy on the movies, thought Tip with surprise. On a job with an operator like Benedict, he would have looked for a Luger, or a long-barrelled .22, the professional's weapon. Benedict was clipping a clumsy-looking chunk of metal to the gun.

'Silencer,' he explained. 'Not really very effective with these, but it does damp the noise down a little.'

Tip was hardly listening. His eyes were glued now to the bright-lit rectangle which was all that could be seen of Oasis Street. Any second now a human being would be framed against that light, an unsuspecting man whose life was going to be snuffed out for no reason at all by him, Tip Brennan. Maybe some business guy, with a wife and kids at home. That was the worst part of this, he decided, not even knowing who the man was. How could anybody expect him to kill somebody he never even saw before.

Benedict handed him the revolver. It felt awkward and heavy in his hand. He should have brought his own gun, that was lighter and he was used to the feel of it. With this thing he'd probably miss the guy altogether.

'Aim for his middle and low,' Benedict instructed. 'That thing kicks a little and you need to give yourself plenty of room for mistakes. Aim just below the belly and you're sure to hit him somewhere.'

He nodded. Aim below the belly, he told himself. Quit thinking about the guy. Concentrate on the gun, think about the gun. It was heavy and it kicked, so you had to aim low in the middle to be sure of a hit.

'You haven't asked who it is,' reminded Benedict.

'You told me no questions, remember?'

'I remember. And good, it's good you didn't ask me. But I'll tell you anyway.

He's nobody, just a wino who's nothing but a pain in the neck to the whole world. Nobody's going to miss him, he doesn't matter at all. That's why I picked him. I don't want the law making any fuss.'

'They'll make some kind of fuss whoever he is,' Tip contradicted.

'No,' said Benedict flatly. 'I'm having him disposed of after you've finished. So nobody will know anything about this except you and me.'

'And the other guys, the ones who are going to dump him.'

'They don't know about you. I'm the only one they'll see.'

A wino. Well, that made sense. Nobody ever knew anything about those guys. They drift into town, foul the place up for a few weeks, even months. Then one day they just ain't there no more. Nobody asks where they are, because the chances are nobody even knew they were there in the first place. They all looked alike those guys, just a big thirst with an empty face. Confidence began to return. This Benedict, he sure thought of everything. A wino was a walking dead man anyway. All he had to do was squeeze the trigger a couple of times and put an end to the walking. And there'd be no squawks.

'He's here,' hissed Benedict.

Tip almost missed him. There, wavering at the end of the alleyway was a man. He took a couple of steps, floundered, then rested a hand against the wall to steady himself. Now he began a cautious procession, one foot after the other. Tip raised the gun, but Benedict put a hand on his arm.

'Too far,' he whispered.

Why didn't he hurry up, thought Tip. It was almost as though he knew what was waiting further down the dark turning. His careful movements could almost be reluctance, an unwillingness to quit even the miserable existence he had. And why wouldn't Benedict let him do it? At that distance it wouldn't be too bad. It wouldn't be quite real, just a man falling down thirty, forty yards away. There wouldn't be — what was the word? impact — yes. There wouldn't be any real impact for the man with the gun. But all the time now he was getting bigger, closer, more real, more like a man. He couldn't be more than ten yards away now.

'Go,' ordered Benedict.

And with the crisp command, all feeling drained away from Tip. No turmoil now, no confusion. Aim for the belly, and low. He saw the revolver come up and point. His finger squeezed and there was a sharp cough as the first slug left it. The wino didn't stop. He kept up that careful step by step. He couldn't have missed. Not at that distance. His finger tightened again and again. The man stopped now, clasping at his middle. Tip couldn't see his face, and was glad. Very slowly, the wino crumpled into a shapeless heap of old clothes.

'Give me the gun.'

Still staring at the dead man, Tip handed over the revolver.

'Now beat it to the car, I'll finish here. Get in the back and don't talk to the woman.'

He nodded and walked away. He didn't look back at the man on the ground. That was over, finished. He was icy calm, and with it was something new, a sensation of unholy exultance. He was a killer, Tip Brennan, and it didn't bother him at all. There was none of the anguish, none of the remorse or pity he'd expected. The whole thing was a push-over. You just point the thing at somebody and squeeze on the trigger. There's a noise and the somebody falls down. You feel nothing, you've seen a hundred guys fall before, from booze or a fist or just fainting. The dead man looks no different, just somebody falling. But he is different, because he's dead, and you killed him. You did that. Tip Brennan. And it didn't mean a thing, not a damned thing. Funny, you think about it for years, even sometimes worry a little, and yet when you come to do it, it's nothing. And you know, you know for sure, you could do it again. Any time.

Benedict watched the dwindling figure of the newly-qualified assassin until he turned a corner and was lost to view. Then he crossed to the dark heap.

'O.K.' he whispered. 'Up.'

The figure stirred and sat upright.

Pulling himself to his feet he grinned in the pale light from a distant lamp.

'How was I? Pretty good, no?'

Benedict grunted.

'Lucky for you,' he said grudgingly. 'If you'd have fouled this up tonight this town would have been too small for you tomorrow.'

The other man spoke again, all the confidence gone from his voice.

'Whatever you say, Mr. Benedict. About the dough — '

'Here. Twenty dollars. You should earn so much for all you had to do.'

Protestingly, the late corpse replied:

'I had to die for it. I ain't supposed to be an actor.'

'Listen pretty boy, and hear me good.'

Benedict placed a huge hand on his chest and grabbed a fistful of clothes, pulling the other close to his face.

'Don't talk about this. Not now, not ever. Tell anybody, just one living soul about what happened here, and the next time you hear a gun go off in an alley you won't get twenty bucks. And you won't have to act dead either. You don't believe it, try me.'

'I believe you Mr. Benedict,' stuttered the other. 'You can rely on me. Listen, ask Mr. Prescott.'

'I already asked Prescott. That's why you're here. And what I said just now, that includes the barber. He won't ask you what you were doing tonight because he knows me and he knows what happens to guys with long noses. So he won't ask, and you won't offer. Ketch?'

'Sure, sure I ketch Mr. Benedict.'

The big man stared into the frightened face thoughtfully for a few moments. Then he released his hold.

'All right, beat it. In three months, if you've kept quiet about this, I'll maybe tell Prescott to put something your way. And you know what'll happen if you don't.'

'Sure thing Mr. Benedict. Er, thanks a lot.'

'Beat it.'

Benedict turned and walked back in the direction Tip had taken. Tip was almost at the car now. At the intersection with the street, he paused automatically, poked his head carefully round the corner to ensure there was nobody around. Then he moved quickly to the car, opened the rear door and slipped inside. At least he'd now get a look at the untouchable dame, he reflected. But the rear seat was empty, and all he could see in front was the back of a woman's head. She didn't turn around, and gave no other indication of being aware he was alive. Who the hell did she think she was, anyhow? He grinned quickly to himself in the darkness. Boy, she wouldn't give him that freeze bit if she knew what he'd just done. She'd give him some kind of play then, all right. Scared, most likely. She'd probably be scared half to death. Although wait a minute. If she was the big guy's woman, she'd have known about death before. Maybe even the big guy himself had knocked off somebody and she knew about it. Yeah. It wasn't likely she'd be scared. Still, there'd be something. Maybe she'd be one of those off-beat kind of dames who couldn't stay away from killers. There was always that kind. Any big-time gunman, there was always lots of dames wanted to get their hands on him. You read about it in the papers, it happened all the time. Well, one day there'd be a few hanging around Tip Brennan that way. It wouldn't break her leg just to say hello. The curled head remained where it was. It needed an effort not to pull her head round and shout at her, sitting there like she was the queen of something. But the top man had said leave her alone and the remembrance acted as a quick brake to Tip. That Benedict now, there was an operator. It took a special kind of man to have a guy knocked off, a harmless nobody. When you took into account the only reason for the killing, which was to find out whether or not he, Tip, would go through with it. That gave Benedict an extra hard edge, a cold remoteness that set him apart from ordinary people. A guy who would do a thing like that, that was a guy to be with. This job they were going to do, whatever it was, that was something special all right. And if he'd had any doubts before, they were gone now. This Benedict would see the caper worked or he wouldn't try it. That was no guy for taking chances.

Aware of a sudden blur of movement in the street, Tip turned quickly to see the big man cross to the car and get in the driving seat.

'It's O.K.' he said over his shoulder. 'Everything's been seen to.'

Tip said O.K. and sat back in the soft upholstery as they moved easily forward. The whole thing seemed wrong. He didn't have any business sitting there in the back of a dark car where nobody could see him. He felt great, he felt fine. You need a good man for some heavy work? That's him over there. The guy in the three hundred dollar suit with the two broads. Sure, that's Tip Brennan. But don't bother him if you're not paying top prices. Tip is a top operator, he don't work for peanuts. That's what ought to be happening. Hey you in front, you know who's sitting back here? Tip Brennan the killer, that's who. In the darkness his lip curled. Who did this big guy think he was, this Benedict? Why did he want that drifter knocked off, back there in the alley? For all the big-time front and all, it wasn't Benedict pulled the trigger, was it? No, that was where he had to stand to one side and let Tip take over. Yeah me, Tip Brennan. And that dame of his, sitting there like she didn't know he was on the earth. Didn't even say hello. Well you wait, you just wait. You'll find out I'm here, that's for sure. People are going to be hearing about Tip Brennan. Always a smart operator, had been for years. Just needed that little break to put him in the top class. Well, he'd made it. Oh sure, he'd do as he was told. He wasn't going to let this run away with him. No sir. To be somebody you have to look like somebody, as well as feel it. And for that you needed all the trimmings. The address, the clothes, the car. All these things cost money, and he was all set for the stake right now. He'd play ball, all right. He'd play ball right through until he got his hands on that twenty grand. Then he could kiss off Benedict and the broad, and really go for the big time. Vegas, Miami, South America. These were the proper places for a big pro, and that was Tip Brennan.

They were clear of Steel City now, and heading across the desert again. Toni was mesmerised by the sameness of the straight, seemingly endless road, and the unchanging desert either side. They hadn't seen another car for almost fifteen minutes, and at this hour it wasn't likely they'd meet much else. She glanced at the speed indicator and saw that it was hovering steadily at ninety. Here she was speeding into the black night, in the middle of nowhere, with two guys she'd never laid eyes on before. Not that there was anything to worry about, she was sure of that. If Benedict had been interested in her that way, he had ample opportunity a few hours earlier at the hotel. To say nothing of the whole of last night. Why, he could have done anything he liked with her at that motel and taken off before anyone else was up and around. Sure, Benedict was O.K. Strange maybe, but not that way. The other one, the young one, she didn't know about him. All she'd seen of him was in the pale lights of street lamps, and even then not a real square look. He could need watching, that one.

He could be almost any kind. Toni hadn't had any opportunity to form one opinion about him. He hadn't even spoken but that was no surprise. Benedict had given her strict orders not to talk to the new man, and no doubt he'd told the man the same. Still, it was funny, sitting there with his eyes eating up the back of your head, and you didn't even know what his name was. When they'd left her in the car back in Steel, she was dying with curiosity to know where they were going, what they were doing. Trouble was, Benedict never told anybody anything. For all she knew, that could have been it, that trip into the darkness between the tall buildings. That could have been the job, the big one, that was going to bring her ten thousand dollars. If it worked. All Benedict had said was that when they were out of sight she was to move to the front seat. She asked whether that meant she was to do the driving and he'd replied icily that when he wanted her to drive he'd tell her so. She'd got up in front as directed, and then realised with dismay that the young one was coming back alone. In the glass, she watched him come up to the car and get in. Where was Benedict? Did it mean something had gone wrong? If it didn't, why wasn't he here with the other one? She wanted to ask, wanted very much to ask, but remembering Benedict's instructions and his cold eyes, she kept quiet. And then he came and all the worry was for nothing. Worry? Why would she worry about Benedict? He was nothing to her. She wasn't worried about him at all, just uneasy. That was it. Uneasy.

And now she was uneasy again. How did she know what these two were up to? Specially that quiet one in the back, sitting there behind her, staring. It had come as a shock when he'd spoken, when he'd said O.K. The voice sounded strained to her, as though something had made him nervous. Or was going to. She glanced sideways at the impassive face of the man behind the wheel. This big man, with all those muscles and obvious strength. He'd slept beside her the night before, slept right beside her in the same

116

bed and never laid a finger on her. Did that sound like a normal man? Then again at the hotel. He'd turned his back while she was changing clothes and gone to sleep. Gone to sleep. O.K. maybe some guys would turn their backs to give a lady a chance for a little privacy. Not many guys, but some. They'd turn their backs, but they'd be thinking about her, wondering. They wouldn't just drift off to sleep that way, as though she wasn't there. No, say what you like, this Benedict wasn't human, wasn't like other men. And this guy in back, whatever his name was, where did he fit in? A thought came into her mind and the blood drained from her face. There was a big police hunt, two, three years back. Two men were wanted. They picked up women, always one at a time and took them somewhere quiet. Then one of them watched while the other one — while the other one —

'What's the matter, you sick?'

Benedict's voice suddenly grated in the night. Toni shook her head rapidly, afraid to speak. Then slowly:

'No, no I'm all right.'

117

Mustn't let him know she was upset. If he thought she was scared it might panic him into doing something. He was slowing down. Oh God, oh please. He was taking a left turn. Again she spoke very slowly, fighting to control the words.

'Why are you doing that? Turning off the highway, I mean.'

'Detour,' he replied. 'There's a town five miles up, regular sleepville. They see a car with three people heading through at two in the morning they'll remember it. And from here on, what we don't need is people remembering us.'

Of course. Only sensible thing to do. Benedict was a smart one, always in there with the think. Silly to worry that way. He can't be stopping. He can't be — .

'Out.'

Benedict was talking to her.

'Out?'

This time she couldn't keep the quaver out of her voice.

'Sure, out,' he said irritably. 'I told you there'd be some sleep for you tonight, didn't I? This is the time.'

She wanted to believe him. Wanted

118

desperately for it to be true. With a hand that shook despite herself, she released the catch on the door, and swung legs that were suddenly made of lead out on the dusty road. Benedict grunted, and slid across to occupy the vacated seat.

'O.K.' he beckoned to Tip with a finger without bothering to look round. 'Up front and wheel this a spell.'

Tip seethed inwardly at being spoken to in such an off-hand way. From anybody else running a caper it might have been all right. They maybe wouldn't know about him. But this guy, he'd *been* there, he'd seen it. You just wouldn't think he'd speak to a man that way.

'Are you coming?'

Benedict wasn't accustomed to waiting, and there was an edge in his voice, an edge Tip knew and recognised from other men, other places. Automatically now he moved, opening the door and getting out. Over the roof of the car he looked at the dim shape of the woman, standing the other side and watching him. What the hell was she looking at? Not that she could see much in this light.

Toni watched with growing relief as the man from the rear seat got in behind the wheel. Scarcely believing there was nothing to fear she got in behind the two men and shut the door.

'O.K. roll,' clipped Benedict. 'You follow this round for about seven miles, keep the town on your right. Then you pick up the main highway a coupla miles the other side.'

Tip released the brake and they were moving. Toni relaxed against the cushions, almost passing out with relief. What a fool she'd been. Like some high school kid out on a hot rod deal with a couple of drunk boys. She wanted to laugh or cry or shout or something. Anything. But these two up front would think she was crazy. They wouldn't understand because none of those things had been in their minds at all, only in hers. Gradually the trembling subsided, and she began to feel drowsy. Well, why not? If these two meant her any harm they'd had plenty of chances already. And she certainly couldn't keep awake all night. She stretched out all along the seat, pulling her skirt down as far as it would go. One of them might look in the mirror, and there was no point in asking for trouble. Within two minutes she was asleep.

7

Toni stirred uncomfortably and shivered. She was cold, and there seemed to be an ache at the back of her neck. Her fingers touched cold leather and with a rush she remembered where she was. It was very early in the morning, judging by the cold brightness through the car windows. She saw that the men had changed places. Benedict was back at the wheel, and the other one was beside him, head slumped forward as though in sleep. The air inside was thick with tobacco fumes, and these two had obviously driven through the night. They would be probably two hundred and fifty miles further than when she fell asleep.

She must look a sight. Where was her bag? Groping towards the floor, she found it and pulled it up beside her. The small hand-mirror did little to reassure her. She was a mess, all right. Taking out a freshener pad she began to wipe off the stale make-up. Aware that someone was watching, she looked up quickly to see Benedict's eyes in the rear mirror. He nodded, but didn't say anything. She smiled uncertainly and nodded back. Then she gave attention to what she was doing. Ten minutes later she felt better. It was still cold, and the crick in her neck hadn't eased, but at least she didn't look like the face on the bar-room floor.

Seeing that the repair job was complete, Benedict half-leaned back and held something out.

'Coffee,' he announced.

Gratefully, she took the flask and poured out some of the steaming liquid. It seemed like a miracle at first, until she reasoned it out. Obviously they'd pulled up somewhere during the night and had the flask filled. But that wasn't the real point. The point was, Benedict had thought to keep some for when she woke up, and she liked that. Whatever else her thoughts about the big man might be, she had to admit when he organised something, he organised it.

'Leave some for him,' he ordered,

inclining his head towards the man beside him.

'Sure,' she replied.

The coffee made its welcome way inside her. She could feel the glow of it spreading over her body. The guy who made this coffee really knew about coffee. But she mustn't take any more, or there'd be none left for sleeping beauty up there. Regretfully, she screwed the cup back in place and passed it across. Benedict took it with a grunt of acknowledgement and poked his elbow at the other one.

'Hey, coffee.'

Tip stirred and passed a hand over his face. His mouth felt foul from the endless cigarettes as he'd eaten up road during his two hours of driving. He was hungry too, and all the guy Benedict was promoting was coffee. A man needed something in his belly besides coffee. He hadn't eaten in over twelve hours, and what kind of a job was this where you had to starve? It wasn't even good coffee, he thought with disgust. Still, at least it was daylight now, and he'd get a look at the broad at last. Emptying the last of the hot drink, he set the flask down on the floor, and felt around for cigarettes. This ought to give him a reasonable opportunity to look round.

Turning he held out the pack. Say, this wasn't bad. This wasn't bad at all. I mean, when you take in this dame had sacked out on a car seat all night, and could look this way. Not bad at all. When she was all dolled up for the races she'd be something to see. No wonder he was supposed to keep his hands off her. This Benedict was protecting a fat investment.

Toni looked at the man who'd turned round. Well, she'd certainly been crazy to think some of the things she'd been thinking last night. This one wasn't bad-looking, if you cared for that type. He'd been around, and when he wanted a woman he wouldn't play any of those funny games to get one. He wouldn't need to. There'd be plenty around willing to come quietly for this tough-looking kid. No, not kid. That wasn't right. There was something old in the face, in the eyes, maybe. About the cigarette, she wasn't sure whether Benedict would like it. Still, he hadn't said anything, so she'd take a chance. Hesitantly, she took one.

'Thanks.'

The car slammed to a sudden halt. Toni and Tip were flung forward, and from his awkward position he banged the side of his head against the instrument panel. Toni only bumped into the softness of the padded seat in front. The two of them looked up in astonishment to see why they'd braked in such a hurry.

Benedict heaved himself halfway over the front seat until he was close to Toni. Deliberately he pulled back his hand and smacked her hard across the face. The force of the blow jerked her head sideways, and immediately the hard hand was back again at the other cheek, slamming her head brutally straight again. She whimpered with pain and fear, staring into the expressionless face above her. Deliberately, he said:

'I told you not to talk to this guy.'

Too stunned to speak, she nodded quickly.

'When I tell you something, you listen.'

The cold eyes withdrew and he slid

down into the driving seat again. Beside him Tip had frozen, waiting for his turn. Jeez, who ever thought the guy would take on that way. All the broad did was say thanks for the cigarette. That wasn't talking at all. Now he'd started the motor again. He wasn't even going to talk to Tip. With annoyance, he found he was relieved. He wasn't afraid of this big man, not really. There were very few people he'd ever been afraid of. And yet there was no denying the feeling of relief as the car rolled forward again. Well, it was between the two of them, the operator and the broad. It was nothing to do with him, not with Tip Brennan it wasn't. A guy who interferes between a man and his woman, that guy is in a heap of trouble and he deserves every bit of it. Behind, Toni sat back, tears streaming down her face. The shock of Benedict's sudden violence had been like being struck by lightning. It had come from nowhere, this unprovoked, unlooked for attack. Her head was singing with the pain of that hard hand, but that wasn't all of it. As she stared into the uncompromising eyes, she'd known, without any doubt at all, that they would not have changed expression if he'd been intending to kill her. He would kill, Benedict would kill, that much was certain. And if she did anything to get in his way, or anything that might interfere with the coming job, those same eyes could be the last thing she would see on this earth. Trembling still, her mind almost numb with fear, she felt the beginnings of hatred for this big man.

In front, knowing his passengers were thinking about him, and knowing too approximately what those thoughts were, Benedict drove calmly on. He'd been hoping for some provocation like that, but not because he wanted to hit the girl. He'd needed the excuse, any excuse, to bring things into focus for her. Till now, all she'd done was sit around in hotel rooms and ride in a car. She knew what she was heading for, or thought she did, but it was vague, formless. It had no shape, no reality. There was some play-acting involved for the girl, and the way things had been ten minutes ago, she might have treated it like play-acting, instead of the cold live thing it was. That was until ten minutes ago. Now it was real. They were no longer to be mistaken for people out on a joyride. They were people with a purpose, people with solid grim reasons for being together, and now she would remember it.

The wide dusty road curved away into the distance. The country had changed in the last hundred miles. Instead of the barren flatness of the desert, there were hills now, small juttings of rock that rose starkly to the shimmering heat of the sky. The early morning chill was gone from the car, and in another hour they'd all feel as though they were being barbecued. Benedict watched the road ahead searching for a suitable flat stretch without too many rocks. This was no time for a broken axle or a busted wheel. That looked all right, up ahead a hundred yards. He slowed down to survey it more closely, decided it would do. Then he swung off the road and on to the smooth dust and scrub.

Tip watched in astonishment as they

bumped gently across country. Any other time he would have asked a question, rule or no rule. But with the memory of the assault of Toni still vivid in his mind he merely watched.

Toni hadn't even noticed what was going on. She was still sitting crouched up, staring at the back of the front seat, scarcely recovered yet from the slapping, not quite believing it had really happened. It wasn't until the car stopped that she looked up. They seemed to be in the middle of nowhere. To the left, the lower slopes of a low range of hills stared impassively at the car. Well, whatever it was all about, at least a girl could stretch her legs.

'O.K. to get out?' she asked, in a dull, lifeless tone.

'Sure.'

Benedict got out too, and flexed his muscles luxuriously. He hadn't realised how many hours he'd been cramped up in the car. The feeling of escape from confinement was a small luxury. He went to the back of the car and dragged out the heavy suitcase. Tip opened the door and stepped out as Toni wandered disconsolately away. She was dragging her feet, and a night on the rear seat hadn't done anything for her clothes, but he could see enough to tell him that was quite a dish. Not that it mattered to him, one way or the other. Dames grew on trees when a man had twenty thousand dollars in his pocket. And they didn't all have an Indian sign put there by a mean operator like this Benedict. No, Tip boy, on this one we pass. He watched with normal interest the neat rolling movement of her hips and rear. Good, very good. But there's better.

'Hey, you.'

Benedict's flat voice from behind interrupted his reverie. He turned to where the big man was bent over the suitcase. What was that he was fooling with? It couldn't be —

'Come and put on one of these.'

He went round. There was no mistake. Benedict was holding out a fancy leather gun belt, western style, with silver decorations and everything. Tip grinned, saw the look on the other's face, and said nothing. The belt was heavy, he found.

He'd never seen one close up before, plenty on television but never close up. They were pretty fancy all right. Look at that silverwork. Why, this must be worth —

'I told you to put it on,' Benedict reminded. 'And get rid of the jacket. Dump it in the car.'

Tip slung the heavy belt around his middle. The first time he secured the big buckle the whole belt sagged. He took it up another notch and this time it was comfortable. Just the same it felt silly, a grown man playing at being a cowboy. There wasn't even a gun. He caught the hostile eyes looking at him again. What was wrong now? Oh, sure. The coat. He pulled it off and walked away, surprised at the difference the heavy belt brought to walking.

Benedict took off his own coat and dropped it on the sand. He'd fixed a similar belt on, and now stood slapping at it to get it comfortable.

We look like two guys walking down Main Street at high noon, thought Tip as he came back. What kind of gag was

Benedict playing, anyway.

Benedict handed over a silver revolver, which looked like the one he'd used before. The one he'd killed that guy with back in Steel. It slid into the holster as though it lived there. This was better. This wasn't so much playing. A gun was a gun, even if it did come in a fancy wrapping. He began to like the weight of it against his leg, like the ready accessibility to his right hand. And the belt may look fancy but it had been made for use. The holster told him that. All round the trigger guard the leather had been cut away, so that once your hand touched the gun, your finger was on the trigger. He felt a boyish desire to draw the gun, see how it felt as it came sliding out. This fast draw bit, all it needed was practice. Some of those guys on the movies, they could toss up a coin, pull the gun and shoot a hole in it before it made the ground. It wasn't all phoney, all that stuff. Tip had read about some of the crack shots from Hollywood in a magazine one time.

'Take this.'

Benedict held out a sack, which

clanked as Tip took it from him. It sounded like a load of empty cans.

'C'm on.'

Benedict had a small wooden case under his arm. They tramped towards the nearest hill.

Toni was beginning to feel better. The clean fresh air was good, and after a couple of hundred yards she decided she ought not to wander any further off. Idly, she wondered what the two men were doing, but didn't much care. Benedict seemed to be carrying a box, and the other one had a bag. The sun glinted suddenly from metal and she put up a hand to shade her eyes. Gunbelts? What did they have in mind, to rob the overland stage? Despite the way she'd been feeling, she couldn't resist a quick chuckle. A quick one, that was all. Whatever they were up to, it would be no laughing matter, that was for sure. Benedict was not the man to indulge in horseplay. They were putting something on the rocks but she was too far away to see clearly. Almost without realising it, she began to walk a little faster.

'O.K. that's enough.'

Benedict turned and walked away. Tip, after a last puzzled look at the row of cans, followed him. The big man counted his paces. Twenty-five. Then he stopped and dragged his toe along the sand, forming a rough line.

'You don't know much about guns, do you?' he queried.

Tip said quickly, 'I knew enough about 'em, last night.'

Benedict grinned sardonically.

'A three-year-old kid could do with a gun what you did last night. What you're going to do now is real shooting. But first, let's see you draw.'

What was this guy, some kind of nut?

'Draw?'

'You heard me. You've seen Matt Dillon do it enough times, now I want to see you.'

Feeling foolish, Tip pulled the gun free and levelled it.

'All wrong,' scoffed Benedict. 'I could have put six slugs in you before you were ready to fire one. Now you have to get this right. We've got all day, and we're going to use as much of it as I think you need. Now to start with, look where your feet are.'

There was no doubt about it, thought Toni. They were gunbelts all right, and over there on those rocks were tins set in a straight line. Maybe this Benedict was president of the Lone Ranger's Local. Or maybe he was just plain loco himself. She sat down on a smooth flat stone and watched.

Tip was over his initial outrage, and beginning to enjoy the game. Funny thing, the way a thing looks easy until you come to try it. That bit with the feet now and the rounding of the shoulders, you wouldn't have thought those little things would make such a difference.

'What's the matter, you got more toes than you need?'

He looked round in surprise. Toes?

'That's a hair-trigger on that gun. You keep stubbing your great fat fingers inside the guard every time you draw, you're going to blow a hole in your foot before you get the thing clear of the holster. Do it like this.'

Benedict showed him in slow motion, fingers flat against the guard until the weapon was nearly parallel with the ground, then curling smoothly inside and round the trigger. Tip nodded, and tried it again. And again.

Toni's first fascination at the sight of two grown men playing cowboys had long worn off. Now she was bored. Getting up she wandered back to the car, and sat inside. On the floor was the crumpled cigarette, the one she'd taken from the young one a second before Benedict hit her. Almost unconsciously her hand crept up to her face. Her jaws still ached, and would for the rest of that day. Picking up the cigarette, she straightened it out and found it hadn't broken. She remembered the heavy gold lighter in the glove compartment. Reaching uncomfortably across she opened it and felt around. The lighter was there, and she snapped a flame to light the cigarette. As she leaned forward again to replace the lighter she noticed something else. Benedict's wallet, the one with the big roll, was tucked under an old piece of rag.

Quickly she turned her head to see if either of the men was watching. They were still doing the Lone Star bit over by the hill, much too engrossed to bother with her. She bit her lip nervously, fingers touching the smooth pigskin. Afraid, she sank back into the rear seat, and sat there undecided for a few minutes. Then she made up her mind, dived forward again and grabbed the wallet. There was no monogram on the outside, that was the first thing she noticed. With fingers that were shaking slightly she opened it. The money occupied one half, a thick crinkly-looking wad of notes that made her mouth water. But she didn't touch it. The other half of the leather pockets was what interested her. Postage stamps, a news clipping and business cards. The clipping was yellowing at the edges, and Toni extracted it with care, fearful of tearing it. It was dated May 17, 1946, and the name of the paper had been something ending in 'GLE'. Bugle? Eagle? Anyway it didn't matter, because the name of the town was missing. There was a picture of a man, and stare as she

138

might, she had to admit finally it couldn't possibly be Benedict, not even after all those years. People change, but not that much. This was a hawk-faced man, with high cheekbones and the skin stretched tautly over the pointed features. The name underneath the picture was Joseph Offerman. The story said that Offerman, 33, had been released from the penitentiary having served six years of a seven to ten sentence for armed robbery. This had been his third conviction and if he should transgress again it would mean life imprisonment. His earlier convictions had been for manslaughter, and assault with a deadly weapon. In addition he had been arrested time out of number for offences ranging from illegal bookmaking to murder. Every time he had either secured an acquittal, or the police had been compelled to drop the case for lack of evidence. There were strong hints about the protection Offerman had received from the Syndicate, intervention on his behalf by leading jurists and other stuff like that. This Offerman had obviously been a mob product, and the mob looks after its own. Toni studied the face again, and wondered what was so special about this piece of paper, almost twenty years old. Why would a man like Benedict want it? If he had a score to settle with this guy, she couldn't imagine him failing to get it over with long before this. And if it was settled, why keep the clipping? Well, there was only one person who could answer her questions satisfactorily and she certainly wouldn't be asking him.

The business cards were all the same. They bore the name of Francis J. Walker, of 2219 Sacramento Avenue, Pine Forks. She read over the name and address, memorising it thoroughly. Then, with great care, she put the clipping and the cards back in the wallet exactly as she'd found them. After a look at the men to see they were still busy, she slid the leather back in its place in the glove compartment.

Joseph Offerman. A man with a record like that must have made a lot of front page news in his time. She kept repeating the name in her mind, hoping it might touch some chord of memory. It was no use. When Offerman had been a prominent hoodlum, she'd been hopping around in pigtails. Well, she was a big girl now. Not that it meant a thing here. She ran her hands thoughtfully down her breasts then to the flat of her stomach. Nothing wrong with her that she could see. And yet so far as Benedict was concerned she might as well be a spare pair of pyjamas. Not that she wanted it any other way, not from that cold, emotionless brute. He'd probably treat her like an animal. The other one though, the young one. He wasn't at all bad. Tough, but what of it? She'd seen 'em all, tough ones, crybabies, criminals, mother's boys. At least he looked alive, and he had thought to offer a cigarette. Yeah, and look what happened when he did. Someday she'd even with Benedict for that.

Tip was getting tired of drawing the gun. He still wasn't as fast as Benedict, and was beginning to doubt that he ever would be. Those guys on the movies, they'd all retire if they could see the greased speed at which the silver revolver leaped into Benedict's hand and pointed at the rocks while his own was still coming up from the direction of the ground. To his sudden surprise Benedict grunted with approval.

'That's good. That's a whole lot better. You're a clear four seconds faster than when we started. You paid attention to what I told you and you stuck with it. We'll get along.'

Despite himself, Tip was pleased. He didn't understand any of it, didn't understand Benedict for that matter. But twenty grand, that he understood. The big guy had said do as he told him, and at the end of the line was twenty grand. So, to Tip, it just followed that he would do exactly that. He would do what he was told. Was doing as he was told. If Benedict said stand on your head, Tip Brennan would stand on his head. That he didn't understand didn't bother him. He was following orders, and that was his ticket to the money. Just the same it was nice the big guy thought he was O.K.

'Here, grab a handful of these.'

Benedict was kneeling down beside the

wooden box he'd carried from the car. He'd prised open the lid, and taken out small boxes. Inside were the heavy slugs that fitted the revolvers. Tip took a couple of the boxes, broke one open.

'Load up. We'll try a little real shooting now.'

The mechanism of the revolver was smooth and oiled. Tip pushed the cartridges in with unpractised fingers, then twirled the barrel the way he'd seen the cowboys do it.

'Never do that,' snapped his instructor. 'With these things you never know. They're not reliable like an automatic. All that fancy stuff is O.K. for the movies, no good for real. Watch this.'

He turned towards the distant tins. Planting his feet apart, he raised the gun above his head brought it slowly down and fired. The bullet smacked into the rock, and a few chippings shot away from the spot. Again the revolver kicked and this time there was a spanging sound as one of the tins flew from sight. The third shot was not dead on target, hitting a tin at the side and spinning it around.

Tip was secretly pleased. The guy was no genius as a marksman anyhow. One hit and one half-hit out of three. That wasn't going to win any medals. He looked expectantly at Benedict, waiting for his turn.

'All right, you try it.'

He nodded, spread out his feet the way Benedict had. Then he reached up with the gun, brought his arm down straight, squinting along the barrel as it straightened out towards the distant tin. There it was, smack in the middle of the sight. Unhurriedly, and with great care, he exerted pressure with his trigger finger. The shining revolver kicked and roared, and the whine of the bullet sang out clearly as it sped harmlessly over the tins. Annoyed, he lined up the barrel again and squeezed. Again, the bullet hummed mockingly along its empty path.

'You're forgetting the recoil,' said Benedict mildly. 'Aim for the bottom of the can and to the left.'

Tip chewed anxiously at his lip. Those things weren't far away and they were laughing at him. He began to understand why he'd been stopped from shooting at that old creep the night before until he could almost reach out and touch him. The third slug splattered against the rock below the target.

'Take it easy,' advised his tutor. 'Don't get worked up about it. You'll never hit a thing that way. Try a few more.'

Suddenly the gun was empty, and the tins still squatted there undisturbed. Tip reloaded. This time the first two shots went the way of the rest. With the third, one of the cans teetered slightly, then fell backwards out of sight. Flushed with triumph, Tip turned to Benedict.

'I finally made it.'

'Not yet. You didn't hit anything. The slug passed over the top. It was close though, close enough for the wind to knock it down.'

Tip didn't believe it. He holstered his weapon and ran to the rocks. Quickly he found his recent target. There wasn't a mark on it. Benedict had been right. When he went back, the big man was squatting on a rock smoking placidly. He was probably going to rub it in.

'Come and sit down a minute. Have a smoke.'

He lit a cigarette, watched the smoke hang lazily in the hot dry air.

'Don't get sore about it,' Benedict told him. 'Listen, I'm doing you a big favour out here today. You're learning something that's gonna save your life one day.'

Tip wasn't convinced.

'All I'm learning is I'm no good with this thing.' He tapped at the gun resting at his side. 'This is gonna save my life?'

The other man nodded.

'If you got brains enough to learn a lesson, it will. Most guys don't get an opportunity like this. First time they find out where they stand, there's some big copper facing them. He knows what he's doing, because he's trained. And the other guy gets dead.'

Disgruntled over his failure, Tip forgot himself enough to ask a question.

'So why should you do me a favour? What's so special about me?'

Benedict hooded his eyes and the friendliness was gone.

'I'll tell you what's special about you,

Brennan. It's this. You're working for me. How good or bad you are with that tool could make the difference to whether I get arrested, or even killed. I've been in this business a long time, and I don't get arrested. I don't even get questioned. You got any brains in your skull, you'll listen to me, watch what I do. Because I know every trick in the calendar, and guys like you don't get a chance with people like me every day.'

'Sure.' Tip knew it was true. 'I didn't mean nothing.'

'That's right. You don't mean a thing. But do as I tell you and maybe someday you'll amount to something. I think you can do it, otherwise you wouldn't be here. Prescott knows better than saddle me with a no-hoper. He knows what'll happen if I'm not satisfied.'

The big man knelt down, scooped a small trench with his finger and dropped the cigarette butt in it. Then he carefully covered it over again, and said:

'Listen, a gun is just a thing that makes a noise until you can shoot straight with it. One time or another, I've worked with

147

every big name in this business. Most of them, anyhow. Big John Weems, Faces Cooper, Rudy Jack Aston. Dozens of 'em. All those guys, and plenty of others, they worked a hundred different ways. They had different temperaments, different ways of doing things. They even had different coloured skins, some of 'em. But the big ones, the good ones, the ones the police could never grab, or very seldom, they had one thing in common.'

He drew his revolver from its holster and ran a hand along it.

'One thing in common,' he repeated. 'They were all expert shots. A gun is a funny thing. It frightens most people, just the look of it. You walk into a bank, a store, start waving one of these around. People get scared. They hand over whatever it is you want. Up to then it's fine, any punk can do it. Then you get outside, and there's somebody don't bust out crying just because you have a gun. Maybe he's got one too, and if you don't stop him he's going to kill you. So what do you do?'

Tip shrugged.

'You kill him first.'

'Wrong. You're wrong twice. In the first place you don't kill him because you can't even hit him. All you hit is some old lady the other side of the street, but you never know that. Because you're stretched out on the sidewalk, bleeding the place up.'

The picture was not appealing. Tip looked nervously away.

'I only meant supposing you could shoot,' he mumbled.

'That's where you're wrong twice,' grated Benedict. 'When you can shoot you don't kill him either, unless you're unlucky. You just shoot him enough so he doesn't bother you any more. Robbery is one thing, shooting is one thing, but a dead cop is something else again. They don't ever forgive you for that. Nobody does. Newspapers, citizens, everybody holds it against you. Even the organisation don't like you if you start killing cops. It stirs everything up, puts on too much heat. Heat holds up the action, and without action nobody can operate. So you don't want to imagine you'll be a big hero if you kill a cop. All you'll be is a big pain to everybody.'

With a final glare at Tip he stood up.

'Now we're going to practice some more. You are going to keep at it until I'm satisfied.'

Tip nodded and followed him back to the improvised range.

In the next ten shots he had two hits, and the grunt of approval he got from Benedict each time was like a salve to his deflated ego. After a while they rested again. The heat of the sun was beginning to make itself felt and Tip was longing for a drink of water. But Benedict showed no sign of letting him off the hook, and he stuck grimly to the job of learning to use the gun. The sand around their feet was beginning to look like a battlefield as the empty shell-cases piled up.

Benedict looked at his strapwatch.

'We'll knock off for a spell, grab something to eat.'

As the two men walked slowly back to the car, Toni felt a quick panic. Supposing Benedict noticed something? Maybe he'd marked the wallet with chalk or something. No chalk on her fingers. Maybe she hadn't put it back just exactly right. He'd notice if it were a fraction of an inch out of line she was sure of that. That clipping too, it had been folded a certain way. She could have refolded it wrong. No that was ridiculous. The cutting was so old, the creases were brown lines and the thing almost folded itself. Still —

The girl looked nervous for some reason, Benedict decided. He wondered about it briefly, then dismissed it from his mind. She was probably wondering whether there was going to be any repetition of the little scene they'd played earlier. Well, that wasn't likely. She'd brought that on herself last time, and she wasn't likely to repeat the mistake. Till now she'd been thinking more and more she was on some kind of Sunday school outing. Now she knew better.

As they climbed into the front of the car, Tip had a quick look at Toni, huddled in the back. That was quite a lot of woman that one. Better not let Benedict catch him looking, though.

The big man settled himself in his seat and spoke over his shoulder.

'Time you got some exercise. There's a lot of empty shell cases out there. Go pick 'em up, all of 'em, and bring 'em back here to me.'

As she opened the door, Toni thought with fury that it wouldn't do the big ape any harm to look at her while he was talking.

Tip didn't glance as she walked away, but he could picture that smooth rolling movement of her hips.

'You said something about eating,' he reminded Benedict. 'My stomach thinks my mouth has a lousy memory.'

'Your stomach is in for a disappointment,' he was told drily. 'We eat where we are. Here.'

He handed over a chocolate bar. Tip looked at it with distaste.

'I'll wait,' he decided.

'Long wait. You'll get nothing else till late tonight.'

Well, he thought, my stomach'll murder me if it doesn't get something to work on.

The chocolate was good. He ate it slowly, remembering how long it was going to be to the next meal. Somebody once told him, if food was short, the great secret was to eat it slowly, chew it all up and make the rations spin out like a four-course dinner.

Toni came back after ten minutes, walked round to Benedict's side and handed over her collection. He grunted and began to count them. The girl watched apprehensively.

'Thirty-one,' Benedict said softly. 'I would have thought you learned your lesson already today.'

With a quaver in her voice she said:

'I — I don't know what you mean.'

'Stupid broad,' he spat savagely. 'I mean I told you to get 'em all. There should be thirty-four. Where's the other three?'

'That was all I could find.'

Her hand was resting on the open window. Benedict placed his hand over hers and pressed it hard against the edge. She gritted her teeth at the pain.

'Thirty-four,' he repeated slowly. 'You bring me thirty-one. That's no good. That's no good at all. Somebody's prints might be on one of those shells. His or mine. Once they have a print it's as good as a photograph. Better. Lots of guys look alike, but no two fingerprints do. Now out there there's three tickets to the penitentiary. Go and find them.'

She nodded quickly, urgently, anything to relieve that awful pressure on her hand. Benedict gave a final squeeze and the agony was gone.

Turning, she stumbled away over the sand.

Tip had watched this performance with detached interest. Benedict was absolutely right, and this time there was no sympathy for the girl. Those shell-cases could be the one thing needed to link them to whatever it was they were going to do. And if anybody happened to get killed it wouldn't be a ticket to the pen. It was a guaranteed pass to the gas chamber. And all for some chuckle headed dame. Without realising it he spoke aloud.

'Chuckle-headed dame.'

Benedict looked at him mildly.

'You think so?'

'Sure. You said yourself, those things

could put us all away.'

The man beside him nodded.

'I said that. But you left them out there in the first place. If you said anything about collecting them up I didn't hear it.'

Tip was silent. There didn't seem to be anything he could say that wouldn't be wrong.

'You didn't even know,' continued Benedict remorselessly, 'how many shots we fired out there, did you?'

'No,' Tip admitted.

'Then don't criticise the woman. She's only stupid at secondhand. They're not her fingerprints. They are yours, and you didn't even give it a thought.'

The voice was like a lash, and Tip knew everything he said was true. One time he would have got angry, but not now. Now he listened, and learned. He didn't like Benedict one bit, but he could recognise the man for a thorough professional with a lot to teach him. They sat in silence. Toni was bent over the loose dry sand, searching for the last of the shell-cases. She'd found two, but didn't dare go back to the car without the other one. As she

155

peered around, the hot salt tears flowed from her eyes. They weren't from the pain in her hand. They were tears of shame that she should be treated like this. Hadn't she done every single damn thing the big gorilla asked of her? And that little creep with him, he just sat there and watched the whole thing. There had been no sympathy, no understanding on his face. He might have been watching television while Benedict was trying to cut her hand in half on that window. Panic began to come into her head. Suppose she didn't find it? What would he do to her? No point in thinking that way, she had to find it, that was all. But where? One scrap of metal in this whole rotten wilderness, it could be anywhere. Some of the others had been half-submerged, trodden in by the men's great feet. But there had at least been something to see. Now there was nothing.

Grabbing a small dried twig that had blown from who knew what distant bush, she began to scratch lightly at the surface sand. Gradually she made a wider circle. There it was, the little beauty. Neatly hidden under a small patch of tramped-down sand that bore the unmistakable imprint of her own foot. Briefly she hated the foot for causing her so much trouble, then made her way back to the car. For some strange reason, which annoyed her, she was glad to have done something that would satisfy the big cold man in the front seat.

There was something like triumph on her face as she handed over the offending shell-cases.

'Three.'

He took them and nodded.

'Good. I left my coat back there. Will you get it before you get back in?'

A request. Not a surly order, but a normal request. Gladly she nodded and went for the coat. There it was lying on the ground. She bent down and picked it up. As she did so, something moved inside it, and a large reddy brown thing scuttled from the folded material on to her arm. Shiny bright eyes stared at her curiously. She felt sick with fear. Although she'd never laid eyes on a fat hairy body like it before, she knew what it was.

Tarantula. If she moved it would be frightened, and frightened it would attack. It was almost certain death, that much she knew. The spider watched her with baleful eyes, which held her fixed with horror.

She was a long time with that coat thought Benedict. Idly he flicked his gaze to the mirror above his head. What was she doing? Standing quite still, with her arm stretched in front of her, fingers clutching the coat. A fit, or what? He got that feeling which spelt trouble.

'Something's wrong,' he said. 'The girl's in a trance or something. Don't make any noise in case you frighten her.'

Tip nodded and opened his door silently. The two men trod on the soft sand and walked slowly towards the petrified girl. She sensed rather than saw them coming, unable to tear her eyes away from the monstrous bloated thing on her arm like an unclean growth. Tip saw it first and his eyes dilated. He grabbed at his companion's arm.

'Say, it's — '

'I see what it is. Keep absolutely still and don't talk.'

The girl was about fifteen feet away, her back half towards him. Carefully, unhurriedly, the big man stepped to his right until the girl was sideways to him. Tip scarcely dared to breathe as he watched Benedict's hand close over the grip of his revolver. Gently he slid it free, raised it above his head. Every movement was smooth and controlled, no jerky actions which might frighten the tarantula. Toni wondered what they were doing. Why didn't they do something? Didn't they know this evil thing was a killer. Desperately she fought down the mounting panic. If anything happened, even if her arm trembled slightly, she was as good as dead. Couldn't they do something? The silver revolver came down in a gentle arc at the end of Benedict's outstretched hand. There was no room for failure now, no excuse for bad nerves. With infinite care, his finger tightened on the trigger. There was a sudden roar, and a faint whoosh of sound as the tarantula disappeared suddenly from her arm. Toni stared, not believing the presence of death had been removed.

'Say, that's the greatest shot I ever saw in my life,' exulted Tip.

Toni smiled half-heartedly and turned to the silent man with the gun.

'I — I — '

Then she pitched forward in a dead faint, still clutching Benedict's coat.

8

Benedict stared at the prostrate figure of the girl. Then he raised his hand almost wearily and wiped away the sweat from his tanned face, sweat that had nothing to do with the sun's fierce heat. Not a bad shot, he admitted, in fact a good shot. He grinned for no special reason, and the grin made his face look quite different. Tip thought he looked almost human for a moment, but some sixth sense warned him not to try cashing in on it. He studiously didn't notice the big man's unexpected display of good humour. What was he doing now?

Benedict knelt beside the unconscious girl and turned her over gently. As the strong sunlight hit her closed eyes she turned her head quickly sideways, and blinked.

'What's happening?' she asked breathlessly. 'Why — oh. I — I remember.'

Her face convulsed with loathing at the

thought of the thing on her arm. She looked quickly down, knowing it to be a waste of time. Knowing the horror was ended, knowing it but scarcely able to believe. For a moment she forgot how scared she was of this big man kneeling beside her.

'You got here just in time, sheriff.'

Her voice faltered over the wisecrack, but Benedict was satisfied. She was all right, this one. She hadn't panicked when she saw death on her arm. She'd probably been hypnotised with fear, but just the same she didn't break down. Plenty of people would have thrown some kind of screaming fit, and they wouldn't all be women either, he reflected. She'd done all right, and now jokes. A terrible joke, but a joke.

'Can you get up O.K.?'

She nodded. 'Yeah.'

With a special effort she forced herself to her feet. For a second she swayed. Benedict's arm was ready to catch her if she fell, but she was determined to manage without it. She even managed a small half-smile.

'About just now, about what you did,' she said shakily. 'You saved my life. Thanks don't mean a thing, I know. But thanks.'

He inclined his head slightly in acknowledgement. Then, satisfied she could make it without him, he turned and went to the car.

Tip watched the scene without comment. Somehow he was glad it had happened. You learn things about people all the time. From nowhere, from peaceful nowhere, they had suddenly found themselves in something, the girl and the big guy. The chips had been way down and they'd been very much O.K. both of them. The woman had shown her stuff in the face of real danger. Danger of a special kind. A dame like that wasn't going to scream the place down the first time she saw a uniform and a badge. And the big man, the operator, he'd known what to do. And more important, he'd done it himself. His nerves had to be made of ice. To be on a caper with these two gave a man confidence.

Without quite intending it, Tip fell into

step beside Toni as she tramped heavily back to the car. He didn't speak, neither did she, but she knew he was trying to provide a little moral support and was grateful.

Benedict was unbuckling the heavy gunbelt.

'You can take that off now,' he told Tip.

Tip nodded and did as he was told. As they stowed away the belts and guns he wondered again what it was all about.

'Here.'

The men looked up. Toni was holding out Benedict's coat. She'd been hanging on to it ever since the tarantula emerged, even when she passed out she'd still been hugging it.

'Thanks. Did you look in the pockets?' Benedict enquired.

For a moment, she coloured with rage. She took the words literally, but he was talking about the — about that thing.

'If there's any more in the other pockets,' she replied 'Don't ask me to shoot them off you. I'd blow your arm off.'

Benedict didn't reply to that. Instead he said briskly:

'O.K., we've got to get moving. You,' pointing to Tip, 'Handle the driving a spell. As for you,' to Toni, 'you better stay in back by yourself and rest a little. You probably have a mild shock.'

They checked around to be certain nothing remained of their stay, and two minutes later, were slowly bumping over the sand back to the highway.

The regular rhythm of the motor soon began to make Toni sleepy. It was hot inside the car. Both men had their shirts showing great black patches of damp, and there was little comfort in the hot dusty air that poured in at the open windows. Her eyes grew heavy, but she was determined to remain awake, if only to show that Benedict she could take it. The lids of her eyes drooped and gradually shut, and she forced them open with difficulty. They were smarting now with the effort and she wasn't focusing properly.

The miles rolled past. Dirty, hot miles of unrelieved boredom for the man at the wheel. First Tip, then Benedict, then Tip again. The strength was fading from the

165

glowing sun now, and some of the air slipping through the interior was almost cool.

On the rear seat Toni stirred and woke up. Damn, she hadn't intended to fall asleep. Maybe they hadn't noticed. Maybe it had only been for a minute or so. She sat upright, feeling the bad taste in her mouth. Neither of the men looked round. She took a peek at the clock in front. Seven o'clock? Impossible. She couldn't have been asleep all that time. The clock must have jammed. But no, she remembered, that wasn't possible. She'd noticed the time when they first reached the place where it had happened. So she'd been asleep for hours. Hours and hours.

'O.K. Turn off left up here.'

Tip started with surprise and almost missed the turn. It was the first thing Benedict had said in over an hour. The feed road was in bad need of repair, and Tip knew a busted spring was the last thing Benedict needed.

'There's a corner up ahead. After we go round, you'll see trees. Drive off the road and get in behind the trees.'

At last. Something different from the endless monotony of the past hours. Those would be the trees over there. Carefully he rolled the car across the uneven scrub and braked.

'O.K. We're here. This is it for a while. Stretch your legs, do what you want, but stay in the cover here. I don't want anybody seeing us from the road.'

Thankfully they all clambered out. Tip put a hand to his back, stiff from cramped hours of driving. What was this place, anyhow? There wasn't a thing here, no sign of civilisation at all. And that meant no food again. This was a great organisation he was mixed up with. No sleep, no food. You kill a guy for no reason at all, only you don't get paid for it. All you get is to make like an imitation cowboy, and nobody talking to you for hours together. Benedict was sitting behind a tree smoking methodically. He seemed to be watching the road, decided Toni. She'd been in a mental turmoil since the big silent man had saved her life. Most men were easy to classify. There were the grabbers and the sneaky ones. If Benedict was one of the second group he was certainly stretching out his sneakiness to the limit. Twice that day he'd hurt and humiliated her. That was enough reason for any girl to hate him till his dying day. Now there was this. You just don't hate people when they save your life, specially when its done the way some hero in a story would do it. True enough, she remembered wryly, the hero in a story would have clasped her in his arms. All Benedict did was let her fall flat on her face in the sand. Still what the hell. It hadn't been a story, it had been for real, and the big lug had done the hard part well enough, the part that mattered.

Time passed and the sun moved down on the horizon, throwing long orange curves into the blackening sky. Tip Brennan and the girl were getting fidgety. If something was going to happen, it ought to happen soon. In their own way, they both began to appreciate the full extent of Benedict's rule about no talking. It hadn't seemed a very irksome instruction when he said it. But keeping silent for hours together was more of a strain than it had sounded.

Away in the distance there was the sound of a heavy motor. Toni heard it first, and ran to the trees to peer into the fast-gathering gloom. Tip watched her wonderingly, then he heard it too and walked across to where Benedict still sat, watching the road with no change of expression.

'Somebody coming,' whispered Tip.

Benedict nodded without looking at him.

The distant hum grew louder, and suddenly a wavering beam of light at the corner announced the approaching vehicle. Toni was getting excited, anxious for any break in the deadly monotony. A big closed truck came into view, crawling round the corner as though afraid of what it might find the other side. The little party behind the trees kept quite still, cut off from view by their cover. The truck motor roared loudly and was silent. The lights went out, on again, then out.

Benedict grunted and got to his feet.

'Stay here, both of you,' he ordered. 'I'll

only be a minute. You can take those bags out of the car.'

He stepped out from the trees and strode the few hundred yards to the waiting truck. As he drew near, the door opened and a man stepped down, yawning widely.

'Right on time, Mr. Walker,' he said.

There was a note of anxiety in his voice, anxiety to please this big man who now stood looking at him with an expressionless face.

'Sure you're right on time, Jerry,' replied Benedict. 'If I couldn't rely on you one hundred per cent I wouldn't have you within a mile of this deal.'

Jerry. He'd called him Jerry, and that was good. That must mean he was in a good mood. It was other times, times when it looked like something might go wrong, those were the times he used that other name, the one that made a man's flesh creep just to hear it again.

'The car's in back,' Jerry reported.

'Naturally. You drove it how many miles?' queried Benedict.

'Like you said, she's been out every

night. Covered near fourteen hundred miles, just the way you said.'

'Pick up any tickets or anything else that would attract attention?'

'No,' protested Jerry. 'I ain't exactly a new boy, Mr. Walker. Everything got done the way you laid it out. Perfect.'

Benedict leaned forward and stuck his face close to the other man's.

'Don't use that word to me, creep. Nothing is perfect. It's guys like you thinking everything is perfect that get their brains scrambled all over the street. Other people's too, if they don't check. So I check. Don't use that word to me.'

'No, anything you say, Mr. Walker.'

'That's right. I thought about you a long time before I decided to use you on this. You're not a new boy, that's true. And that was what worried me. You're old. Old and rusty.'

'Not much over fifty,' retorted Jerry. 'And I'm as spry as any of these young punks nowadays.'

'I think that's right. I think you can do it. You're going to have to do it now. Get the car out.'

Jerry scuttled to the rear of the truck and opened the doors. Then he struggled with two heavy ramps that he pulled from the interior to form a crude roadway down to the surface of the highway. Hopping up inside he started a motor, and began to back a large convertible down the slope.

Tip and Toni were standing side by side watching in amazement. There was no chance of Benedict overhearing at that distance, but the man's influence was such that it didn't occur to either of them to speak. The convertible bumped gently down, and away from the truck. Jerry cut the motor and came back to Benedict.

'O.K.?' he asked anxiously.

'Wait here.'

Benedict walked back towards the trees. He didn't hurry himself, and Tip and Toni watched eagerly, waiting to hear what was going on. The big man ignored Toni and said to Tip.

'Bring the car down to the truck.'

'What about me?' demanded the girl.

Slowly he turned his head as though

172

remembering her presence for the first time.

'I told you to stay here. Till I tell you different, that's what you do.'

She nodded dejectedly and stepped away from him.

Tip went to the car and got in. He swung it round in a wide curve to head back to the highway. By the time he arrived Benedict was already there, waiting.

'Drive it up inside the truck. Then stay in it until he says out. Got it?'

'Got it.'

'I won't see you for a while. You'll be with him now for tonight. His name is Jerry, and you don't have any name at all. You don't come from anywhere, you don't know anything. Especially about me and the woman. That's what I've told him, that's what I'm telling you.'

'Is it O.K. to talk to him?' queried Tip.

'Talk all you want. But remember what I said. I'll see you tomorrow some time.'

''Kay.'

Tip eased the car forward carefully and nosed onto the ramps. One minute later he and the car were engulfed in the dark of the truck.

Alone by the trees Toni watched the car, their car as she couldn't help thinking of it, as it disappeared inside the black hulk of the truck. If all they were doing was switching cars, it seemed an awful complicated way of doing it. All that was necessary was for the other man, the truck driver, to drive the second car out to the meeting place and make a straight trade. Still, if that was the way Benedict had decided to do it, there had to be some kind of reason. He didn't do anything wacky, she had to give him that. Hey, the driver was shutting the doors with the other guy still inside. Now he was talking to Benedict again.

'Your house guest is worn out,' Benedict said. 'He needs food and a good night's sleep. Do like I told you, and keep him out of sight. I'll drop around tomorrow.'

'What time tomorrow, Mr. Walker?'

The big man smiled thinly.

'If I told you that you'd be ready for me wouldn't you? I'll just arrive when I feel

174

like it. Don't be doing anything I wouldn't like when I get there. Especially anything to do with a bottle.'

'Honest, that was years ago. I ain't touched the stuff in years. You can trust me, Mr. Walker.'

'Oh, I trust you, Jerry. Because if I have any trouble with you, I'll pass along the word when you're holed up. It's been a long time, but there's people would still like to look you up. Kind of renew old acquaintances.'

Jerry blanched.

'Jeez, you don't have to threaten me that way, Mr. Walker. Don't do that will you please? It makes me break out in a sweat. Didn't I do everything you wanted? And do it right?'

'Very good, Jerry.' Benedict poked him with a big forefinger. 'You're doing very good. Keep doing it and I may forget the whole thing. And don't forget you got plenty to do at first light tomorrow.'

He turned and walked away. The stocky man called Jerry stared after him with hatred. He ought to knock him off right here and now. It would be easy and it would be a pleasure. Then what? He'd still have to take care of the other guy, the one in the truck. He might have a gun. And there was somebody else too, back there in those trees, maybe more than one for all he knew. That was the hell of this whole deal. A man didn't get told anything, except the next thing he had to do. And in his case, he certainly had to do it, whatever it was. This pig who called himself Walker, he was holding all the cards.

Jerry shrugged and sighed. Then he climbed up into the driving cab and backed the heavy truck around until it was pointing the way he'd come. A few moments later it disappeared round the corner and was gone.

Toni watched the big figure advancing towards her. She was dirty and hungry and fed up. If Benedict said there was plenty more driving to do, this was where she got off. There wasn't that much money in the world a girl should put up with this kind of treatment. He could keep his lousy ten grand. Ten grand. Ten thousand dollars. The figures rose in her mind and hung there, a tantalising green colour. What was she thinking? She was thinking crazy, that was what she was thinking. Ten thousand dollars was a sum she'd never get close to again. There was just one chance if you were lucky, and this was the time. Anyway, it was a lucky thing Benedict couldn't see inside her mind.

'C'm on,' he said briefly. 'We have to get going.'

He hoisted the heavy bag and pointed to the other one. Toni picked it up. Obediently, she walked along beside him.

'I know you said no questions,' she began haltingly. 'But I don't think I can take much more of this without some food. Do we get to eat?'

He didn't bite her head off. Instead he replied:

'One hour from now you can eat till you drop.'

Good. One hour was practically no time at all. It probably meant they were within fifty miles of wherever they were going. Not that it really mattered what the place was called. Just so they'd heard of food. The second car was a disappointment. A three-year-old convertible it looked as if it had driven many hard miles. They settled inside, and were soon heading back along the road to the main highway. Toni was all set for another silence, but Benedict seemed to want to talk for once.

'You ever hear of Pine Forks?' he queried.

'No. I don't think so. One place is like the last place,' she answered.

'We're not talking about the last place. We're talking about Pine Forks. That's where I live. My name is Frank Walker, and you're my sister Iris. You had some bad luck, married a guy who was no good. He went off and left you and you've been ill because of it. I've been up to San Francisco to bring you back to Pine Forks for a while. Till you pull yourself together a little. What's your name?'

The sudden question took Toni by surprise, but she'd been listening carefully.

'I'm Iris Walker,' she returned.

'How can you be Walker?' he contradicted. 'That was before you got married.'

She thought quickly.

'The marriage is something I want to forget. I want to forget him, the marriage, everything. I don't ever want to hear the name again. See,' she held up her left hand. 'I don't even wear a wedding ring.'

He looked at the hand, looked back at the road. A slow grin crept over his face.

'Iris, girl, it looks like I acquired a sister with sense in her head. O.K. you're Iris Walker.'

From Benedict, such praise was equal to the keys of the city.

'Thank you, Frank.'

She wanted to say more, anxious to impress him with how smart she could be, just given a chance. But she decided against it. Let it lay. Don't hammer it into the ground. Instead she asked a question.

'Who am I going to have to explain all this to?'

He shrugged.

'Probably nobody, but I don't believe in taking chances. I have a small house in Pine Forks, and neighbours know I'm kind of a loner. They don't bother me much. But I spread this tale about collecting my sister. It covered my absence for several days and also accounts for you turning up at the house if anybody sees you.'

'Am I supposed to know what business you're in?'

Benedict shook his head.

'No, we haven't seen each other in years. Anyhow, you're not very smart. Look at the dumb thing you did marrying a guy like that. So you wouldn't be expected to know anything much about me.'

The girl digested this.

'I take it there isn't any Mrs. Frank Walker?'

'Right.'

Ahead on the flat straight highway, she could see a glow of light against the black of the night sky. That would be Pine Forks where Iris Walker had come to lick her wounds.

'One thing else I ought to tell you,' her new brother cut in on her thoughts. 'You're expected to be a good-looker, you know, make an impact. So no slouching around. You wear those duds you bought back there, and keep plenty of stuff plastered on your face.'

'Whatever you say.'

A few minutes later they drove into town. Toni was surprised to see so many people out on the streets. A number of stores were open, too. All the windows were gaily decorated, and there were coloured lights hanging everywhere. Benedict pulled into the kerb.

'I'm going to pick up some food,' he told her. 'Stay in the car, but don't be afraid to let anybody see you if they look interested.'

After he'd gone, she opened her purse and began applying more make-up to her face. Might as well get down to this Iris Walker stuff right away. Benedict wasn't gone long. He came back with his arms full of paper bags.

'I'll take those, Frank.'

She took them from him and arranged them round her feet on the floor. Benedict got in.

'I see you went right to work in the art

department,' he observed. 'We might get along, you and me.'

She made no reply, and they drove out of the town centre, heading into a residential neighbourhood. Sacramento Avenue was a wide quiet street with neat small houses spaced out at regular intervals. 2219 looked just like all the rest as Benedict nosed the car up onto the concrete strip leading to the garage.

'I'll put it inside later,' he announced. 'Let's get all this stuff in the house.'

They found they could just manage everything in one trip. Benedict produced a key and they went inside. The girl felt a quick pang. It was a long time since she'd been inside an ordinary house. This was nothing like the place she'd grown up in, but there was somehow the same kind of atmosphere. It took her mind back immediately to those days when they'd been kids, she and her brother. What was it, a million years ago, two million?

She wandered around, looking at everything. There wasn't much furniture in the place, she noticed. Still if the big man lived here alone he wouldn't need a lot. You could tell there was no woman in the house, and yet he seemed to be a tidy man. Usually you'd find a hogpen when a man led this kind of life, but Benedict had kept the worst of the muddle at bay. The kitchen needed a lot of alterations, but it looked good to her. As she stood musing out there the swing door was pushed open, and Benedict came in carrying all his purchases.

'I'll get rid of the bags,' he announced, 'You get moving with some food. And plenty of it.'

He marched out again. The girl looked around at her new province. She hadn't been in a real kitchen since — oh — well since the flood. Hesitantly she began to unwrap the packages.

9

Lulled by the monotony of the cushioned bouncing inside the big truck, Tip was resting both hands on the wheel his head on his arms. Twice in the last few minutes the movement had stopped. That probably meant traffic and they were in a town. Could be the town where it was going to happen whatever it was. The movement stopped again, and he waited. This time the pause was longer than before. Maybe a jammed traffic light. A sudden noise from behind brought him quickly to the surface. A thin crack of light appeared, and banging noises announced that the rear doors were being opened. He twisted on the seat and looked out into what seemed like the inside of a warehouse. The driver of the truck appeared and waved him to come down. He opened the door and stepped out, picking his way carefully until he was able to jump out.

'Gimme a hand with these doors, huh? Don't want anybody nosing around that car of yours.'

He helped secure the doors again. At the same time he was studying the guy Benedict had called Jerry. He wasn't very tall, but built husky enough. The only thing he couldn't understand was why Benedict had to go and fix up somebody this old. Tip wasn't very good at assessing ages but this guy was older than most you'd find on a thing. Like old enough to be somebody's father for instance.

When they were finished, Jerry said:

'Tell me you're hungry and tired. Right?'

'Right.'

'Follow me, and we'll get something done about your stummick.'

Trailing behind him, Tip was trying to place the special twang he could detect in Jerry's voice. Tip didn't know much about that kind of thing either, but he knew enough to be positive the old man had not started out in life this far south-west. He talked more like somebody from the east. New York or like that.

185

Busy with these thoughts he took time to notice his first guess had been wrong. This was no warehouse, not now anyway. More likely to be just a garage for parking big trucks like the one he'd arrived in, Jerry led him up a flight of rickety wooden steps and into a small, dark room. Heading straight through, Tip found himself in a narrow box of a room, with a table, a couch and a couple of chairs. There were no windows.

'Ritzy,' he sneered.

Jerry looked at him thoughtfully. Tough, he decided. Tough, but green. A newcomer to an operation such as Walker was planning. Not that Jerry knew what the plan was, but he knew the business, knew how to recognise an operator of Walker's class. This kid with the hard eyes didn't seem to have the class. Still, we all have to start someplace, he decided philosophically. There had to be something in this young punk that Walker needed, or he wouldn't be here.

'You ain't seen much of the world,' he replied mildly. 'I can think of times, plenty times, this would have looked better to me than any Ritz.'

Although the tone was mild, Tip's ears were sharp enough to detect that this character wasn't trying to butter him up. He thought, with quick resentment, that this faded has-been considered himself as good as Tip Brennan.

'I never been flat on my face, if that's what you mean by seeing the world,' he said nastily.

Jerry chuckled, but there was no smile in the bright eyes that looked at Tip steadily.

'Ain't what I mean,' he countered. 'In a few years, if you live that long, you'll learn to recognise a place like this. Look around.'

Tip stared round with quick distaste.

'A dump,' he decided.

'Boy, I ain't supposed to fight with you, so mind your tongue,' Jerry warned him. 'Now you're going to learn something, so listen. You're on the run, see? Where do you hole up?'

Tip wasn't in the mood for playing games.

'You tell me,' he shrugged.

'I'll tell you. You pray for a place like this. See, no window. Only one door. Other side of the door, a room. Only one way into that room, and that's up a flight of steps that squeaks like a dame the plumber caught in the bath. Nobody's getting in here, just nobody, without you know it from miles away.'

Tip took this in, and had another look at his informant. Maybe this guy could tell him something after all.

'I see what you mean,' he admitted.

'That's only half of it,' continued Jerry. 'No window means you can have the light on any time and nobody knows there's anybody here. Not even somebody in the next room.'

It wouldn't do to let this ancient know-all have it all his own way.

'Sure, you're tucked up like a bug. You can hear 'em coming,' he retorted, 'But so what? The place may as well be a cell. Once they come, they got you all sewed up.'

Jerry only grinned again.

'You, yes,' he agreed. 'And you'd deserve it, 'cause you don't use the eyes you were born with. Look.'

He kicked away the tattered rug on the floor. Beneath was a square trapdoor, big enough for a man's body to pass through.

'Leads clear under the foundations. You wind up in a cellar the other end of the block. They built this town on stilts, account of we get a heap of surface floods when the big rain comes.'

Tip wondered how he ever got in this crazy argument. Now he flopped into one of the chairs.

'Okay,' he said resignedly, 'I didn't have any cards. How 'bout that grub?'

'There's a delicatessen right across the street. They'll think I'm staying on here late. I do that sometimes lately. There ain't any need, but the idea was it wouldn't be out of the ordinary for me to start wanting food there when I needed it for you.'

This time Tip was impressed.

'How long you been doing that?' he asked.

'Most of two months now,' came the reply. 'When you got something big going, you have to plan everything. I'll be back with the grub. You stay in here.'

Jerry went out, and the younger man lit a cigarette. Two months of setting up unnecessary food, just to avoid attracting attention when the time came. That was thinking. That was the kind of planning that had to be behind a big operation. And that was where you needed somebody like Benedict. At every turn, he was finding the kind of organisation a man like him never thought about. Back in Steel City, Charlie Prescott was the boss man, and Tip had always looked up to him as being smart. But Charlie wasn't really so smart, he could see that now. Charlie could never begin to set up anything like this. He got on top in the old days, when it was no more than kill or be killed. Now he stayed up there by hiring guys like Tip Brennan to stamp on any signs of opposition. Charlie was tough, and what's the word? Ruthless. Yeah, that was Charlie. But Benedict was in a different class, and it had been a lucky day for Tip when he showed. He'd often thought about going out on his own some day, but with nothing like this in mind. It would have been shoot grab and run stuff. Amateur night, once you'd seen a big pro like Benedict close to.

After a few minutes Jerry came back with a steaming tray. Tip's stomach rumbled gratefully as the appetising smell floated to his nostrils.

'Try that for size,' suggested Jerry.

He sat in the other chair and watched while his visitor wolfed into the food. When Walker said this guy was hungry, he was making the understatement of the year.

Tip got rid of everything in sight in record time. With a smacking sound he swallowed the last of the coffee and sat back.

'I don't remember when I was that hungry,' he said.

'I imagine,' returned Jerry drily. 'When'd you eat last?'

Tip was about to reply when he remembered.

'Sorry,' he shook his head. 'I ain't supposed to tell you a thing.'

He was surprised to find Jerry laughing.

191

'Good, good. Never liked a talkative man. A man who talks is liable to say the wrong thing in the wrong place. Once that happens, somebody's gonna wind up the wrong side of them stone walls. So I'll just ask you one more question.'

Tip's eyes narrowed suspiciously.

'What's that?'

'Can you play pinochle?'

* * *

Toni watched anxiously as Benedict pushed his plate away.

'Pretty good,' he admitted. 'Now we better get some sleep. Got to make an early start tomorrow.'

She nodded and got up to begin stacking the dishes.

'Leave that,' he ordered.

She nodded again and went out of the room to the stairs. She didn't know yet where she was supposed to sleep. Benedict walked up behind her.

'I fixed up the room on the right,' he informed her. 'It ain't much, but it won't be for long. And it has the only good mirror in the house.'

As she opened the door to go in, he spoke again.

'Hurry up and get clear of the bathroom will you? I want to take a shower.'

'O.K.'

The room was nothing special, he'd been right about that. Her bag lay on the narrow bed, and she began automatically to unpack.

In the room opposite, Benedict stripped off his jacket and tie. Everything was all right. Correction. Everything seemed to be all right. Nothing was ever all right until the money was in your hands, and you were long, long gone. But up till this, O.K. He grinned inwardly at the trick he'd played on that Brennan guy the previous night. A fake killing, yet. Still, it had been necessary. It would have been no time to find out Brennan had nothing inside when he was standing next to him facing armed police. If it came to that. With reasonable luck that wouldn't happen, but you can't leave things like that blindly to luck. The girl too, she'd handled that bit with the spider A.O.K. And guts weren't the only thing she had on the ball. He thought of the curves of her body, the flat tight stomach, and the way her hips rolled as she walked. She was only across the passage, not fifteen feet away. No. He'd meant what he said to her that first time. Any girl on a caper like this would take it as part of the deal that she'd have to put out for the top man. But he didn't want it like that. He regarded it as the same thing as buying it in a cathouse. There was nothing voluntary on the part of the woman, and without that there could be no excitement.

Toni came back from the bathroom and went into the bedroom she'd been given. This Benedict wasn't human, that was for sure. Annoyed, she took off the rest of her clothes and stood looking at herself critically in the long mirror. Was there a new thickness there at the hips? She ran her hands carefully down. No. No sagging either at those vital thirty-six inches. Turning sideways she arched her back and admired the silhouette. Hands on hips, she looked suddenly at her slim

194

arm, and chilled at the memory of the thing crouching there a few short hours earlier. If it hadn't been for that big man opposite —

Benedict stood under the shower, feeling the needle spray soothing away the tiredness. He turned the control to full cold and shuddered at the sudden bite of the water. When he'd had enough he turned the shower off, lifted the towel from the rail outside and had a few brisk rubs. Then he pulled back the curtain and stepped out.

The girl was standing there, smiling mockingly. She looked as though she'd just stepped from the shower too. Only she didn't even have a towel.

'I wonder if I could borrow a cup of sugar?' she asked.

Benedict threw away the towel. Now it was all right.

'Well, now, honey,' he said softly, 'This really seems to make it your idea, doesn't it?'

10

Five miles outside Pine Forks the bright glow of lights might have been mistaken for a small town. In its own way, it was a small town. A travelling town of people and animals, the Gorman Brothers Grand Circus. The gay trailers and tents were silent now after the day's hectic excitement of preparation. Circus folk have to turn their hands to more kinds of work than the public see in the ring. There are animals to tend, equipment to repair, the endless splashing on of bright gaudy paint. Some kind of schooling to provide for the little ones, washing, cooking, make new costumes and repair the old. Keep supple for the current act, try out innumerable routines for the new act that's going to knock them dead when it's perfected. There are neighbours to help out in sickness, last minute programme adjustments, the same old arguments with the bandleader about the timing for the specialty number. The continual pandemonium of keeping to the schedule, tearing down and packing up after the last performance. Riding dog-tired through the night, because that's the only way to have any chance at all of being ready in time for the next town.

The next town was going to be Pine Forks, and even by the high standards of Gorman Brothers — Fifty Years in the Sawdust Ring — the preparations had been intensive. Plenty of outfits would have liked the solid business, to say nothing of the widespread publicity that would attend the Grand Centenary Celebration at Pine Forks. Exactly one hundred years ago, the first settlers had sunk their picks in that unfriendly ground and sworn to make something of the place. The settlement had had its ups and downs, mostly downs the first fifty years. What with Indians, outlaws, drought and the big hot winds, the place had been abandoned more than once. But gradually the people had won, and Pine Forks was solid enough today. Solid enough to generate a sensitivity to any suggestion it hadn't been long established. The City Council had hired a historian to research around and get some idea just how long Pine Forks had been a settled community. They had been hoping secretly for some evidence of Spanish occupation that would validate a claim to three centuries or more. But the historian was an honest man and they had to settle for one hundred years. No precise day and month had been established, so it had been agreed by mutual consent that the most suitable time for the celebrations would be at the end of summer, and now the show was about to start. A committee of townspeople had wanted to declare a local holiday for all stores and offices for the day, but the City Council had resisted the suggestion with commendable firmness. After all, when you have regard to all the time and effort that was going to be put into this thing, and all for no reward other than the satisfaction of knowing they were doing their public duty, it seemed a little hard to expect the members of the Council to agree. To ask them to close down the stores and offices, *their* stores and offices, just at a time when the public was in a gay mood, a spending mood, well it did seem just a little hard on those public-spirited men.

So there was to be no holiday, but naturally you could expect some leniency over such matters as being late on the job and so forth.

And so, the circus. Gorman Brothers were to open the day's events with a grand parade through the town, just the way it would have been all those years back. Well, at least a few years back. The streets would be decorated and gay, and then Gorman Brothers would come through with the whole works, clowns, elephants, pretty equestriennes, gibbering monkeys. The whole bit. The City Council had made it clear they would not tolerate any cheapskate show, and Gorman Brothers had got the message. All that day the site had been a turmoil of frantic hither and thither, quarrelling about precedence — 'I never followed no performing dog in my life' — concern about the strong man's sudden stomach pains, wails at the discovery of some unexpected rip in a favourite costume. The frenzy had persisted into the evening, gradually losing momentum, and now at one thirty in the morning there was silence. Circus silence, which is not a total absence of sound. It is the creak of ropes and canvas in the light breeze, the occasional snicker of a horse, the stamp of a restless elephant's foot. But rarely any human noises.

There was an alien noise now, the irritable whirr of a starter and the deep growl of a motor firing. Disturbed, a cage of monkeys chattered with frustrated rage at being woken, then again silence.

Asleep in his plush caravan, Pat Gorman stirred and grunted. For a long time there was no more noise. Then a rapping, an insistent rapping at the door.

'H'm. Huh?'

Gorman rolled over, blinked and came awake.

'What is it?'

The door opened and a husky man stood looking at him. With quick alarm in his voice Gorman said:

'Fire?'

'No, Pat, it's no cause for panic like that. Sorry to wake you, but you said — '

'C'm on in, and don't be sorry. You did right. With this big thing tomorrow I have to know every little thing.'

The big man came in and closed the door.

'It's that guy Bushman, you know the one we hired on back at — '

'I remember. What about him, Ed?'

'He's gone.'

'Gone?'

There was disbelief at first, gradually changing to belief.

'Gone?' roared Gorman. 'Just gone?'

'Yeah,' confirmed Ed unhappily.

To quit the circus the night before a parade is the same thing as deserting your post in face of an enemy attack.

'The money?' asked Gorman quickly.

'O.K. I checked that right away. Nothing missing there.'

Gorman nodded and bit his lip with perplexity.

'Anything else missing?'

Ed shrugged his big shoulders.

'I can't say definitely nothing. But

201

nothing big, that's for sure. He may have gotten away with a few bits and pieces, but nothing that ought to matter.'

'Don't get it,' muttered his boss. 'If he didn't take anything valuable, why leave?'

'I've been asking myself that question for near thirty years, Pat. You know how these guys are, these drifters. They're not real circus, not like you and me and those others out there. What do you want me to do? I could wake a few of the guys and get after him.'

Gorman thought about it.

'What's the time?'

'Almost four.'

Four o'clock in the morning, and this was no day to be chasing a runt like Bushman.

'No, let it go,' he decided. 'We all had a tough day yesterday, and there's another one coming up. Let me know in the morning if anything's gone. If it is we'll tip off the chief in Pine Forks, and let the law take care of him. Go get some sleep.'

Ed nodded.

'Whatever you say, Pat. Sorry I woke you up.'

'G'night.'

The door closed behind the big man and Pat Gorman flopped heavily back in his bunk. A man didn't have enough problems in this world. He had to go hire himself one named Bushman. How could you get circus from a guy like that? He probably crawled out from under a bush in the first place.

The thin, worried looking man named Bushman sat cradling a cup of steaming coffee and watching the door anxiously. There were a few other customers in the all-night diner, mostly truck-drivers grabbing a few minutes rest before the grind across the desert. Nobody paid any attention to the nondescript figure in the corner. He in turn had no eyes for anyone else in the place. All his attention was focused on that door. If he hadn't lost his mind, and he was beginning to wonder about that, a man would look through the glass panels at five o'clock exactly. Bushman had never laid eyes on the man, but he would sip at his coffee when the other arrived, and then the newcomer would make his move. It sounded crazy,

O.K. it *was* crazy, but that was the way it had been set up and that was the way Bushman would do it. There was nothing crazy about the torn half of a one hundred dollar bill he was carrying in his pocket. All his life he'd been a drifter, roaming around from one place to another, doing whatever came along that would earn enough money to keep him in food and a place to sleep. The man at Jacksonville had changed all that.

Now, sitting in the smoky atmosphere of the diner his mind harked back to that strange encounter. Well, he hadn't loused it up. He'd done exactly what the big feller had said, and now he was here to collect. And he was wanting to get on with it and be on his way. If those guys from Gorman's caught up with him they'd beat him to a pulp. Walking out at a time like this, that was a bad thing to do to circus people. They weren't going to shake him by the hand and tell him to forget the whole thing.

Wait a minute, there was a guy out there. Bushman picked up his cup slowly and made a great show of swallowing.

The man outside nodded, then jerked his head to one side. Bushman, despite himself, felt a momentary panic. How did he know what was going to happen to him out there? The whole thing was goofy anyhow. Maybe he ought to sit tight, leave when some of these truckies did. Then he thought back to the last time he'd seen the big man, and knew he'd have to go through with it. Slowly he got up and walked out through the door.

'Over here.'

The stranger was about his own height, but much huskier all round. He was also several years older. Bushman walked up to him.

'You Bushman?'

He nodded.

'And you?'

'Never mind that. Did you get everything?'

'Sure. Just like he said, the big feller.'

'O.K. Where is it?'

'In the car.'

He pointed to the old jalopy he'd saved for carefully out of the starvation wages the Gorman Brothers paid him. Not that he'd been worth any more.

'If that thing really moves, drive it over next to mine. The blue one.'

Bushman climbed into the old heap and started her up. Jerry watched him curiously. You had to hand it to Walker. He seemed to make everything and everybody tick like a piece of clockwork. And nobody would ever connect that derelict and his travelling trash-can with an operator like Walker.

It took no more than three minutes to transfer the stuff from Bushman's car to Jerry's. When they were finished Jerry said:

'You did O.K. Now you only have one more thing to do. Get that junkheap moving as far as the nearest railhead away from Pine Forks. Go where you like. I ain't asking and I don't want you to tell me. Just get on the first train out and keep going.'

'Sure thing, mister. You can rely on it. The big feller told me what to do, and I listened to every word. I sure as hell don't want no trouble with that one.'

Jerry seemed satisfied.

'Get in my car a minute. We don't want any nosey people seeing what goes on.'

In the car. Bushman produced the grubby envelope in which he'd been hoarding his half of the hundred dollar bill with loving care.

'Here's my half,' he announced.

Jerry took out a pigskin billfold and extracted the other half. Bushman took it with trembling fingers. Now, at last, it was more than just a big hope. This was reality. Jerry watched the greed on his face with secret contempt. A piker. A lousy piker. Nonchalantly, he pulled out another bill and handed that over too. The little man beside him had never seen so much money at one time.

'Satisfied?' demanded Jerry.

'Sure, sure I'm satisfied. Say, this is a great day for me — '

'Give it back.'

'Huh?'

Bushman clutched the bills against his chest desperately. They couldn't do this, they couldn't just cheat him this way. Jerry clicked his fingers impatiently.

'C'm on, don't stall.'

Bushman blinked back a tear.

'You can't do this. The big feller promised me. He said — '

Jerry sighed with exasperation.

'Look, how far do you think you'd get? Look at you, look at that thing you call a car. When anybody who looks the way you look starts tossing around century notes, somebody hollers for the law.' He tapped at the wallet. 'I have it all here in fives and tens. That way you should keep out of trouble.'

'Oh.'

The little man's relief was almost pathetic. They weren't going to double-cross him at all. It made sense, what this guy was saying. Reluctantly he released his hold on the bills, and Jerry stuffed them away. Then he pulled out a much thicker wad and passed it across.

'Count it,' he invited.

This was better still. There was more for a man to feel. Bushman riffled excitedly at the pile. They'd made a mistake, he thought with quick cunning. There was twenty-five dollars too much here. Should he tell, or just put it in his pocket? No, maybe they were playing a game with him, testing him out.

'You made a mistake, mister. There's two-twenty-five here,' he pointed out.

'No mistake. The extra quarter is for your rail ticket. Spend it all. You hear me?'

'I hear you. Spend it all. Sure.'

Jerry leaned closer to him casually, and brought up his right hand. In it was a thin wicked-looking knife. Before Bushman could move the point was scratching at his wind-pipe.

'Now just let's go over it once more,' said Jerry softly. 'What is it you have to do, now?'

Stuttering with terror, Bushman jerked out his instructions. As he finished, the evil shining blade slid away from his throat.

'O.K. Bushman. Don't let's ever hear your name round here again. Now take off.'

He stumbled from the car teeth chattering with fright. He had to support himself by leaning against Jerry's car as he tottered round to his own.

After a couple of false starts the old

engine coughed, and Bushman's jalopy moved jerkily out on to the road and away. Jerry watched until it was out of sight. He didn't think there was any need to worry about that guy. They'd never see him again. Now he'd better get back to town before there were too many people around.

11

Toni stirred and stretched luxuriously.
Half awake she realised suddenly there
was someone watching her. Sleepily she
opened her eyes. Benedict, or Frank
Walker, or whoever he was was standing
beside the bed. He was already dressed in
a faded shirt and old trousers. She
smiled.

'You're up early, honey. Come back to
bed a while.'

'Up,' he said tersely.

She pouted.

'Aw, honey, that's no way to talk to me.
Not after last night.'

Benedict sighed.

'That was last night, that was for kicks.
This is business. Up.'

She wanted to argue, partly from
vanity. Wanted to see what difference the
night had made to her relationship with
this man. The man she'd imagined was
so cold, she remembered. How wrong

can a girl be? But there was nothing in his voice, nothing on his face, to suggest anything had changed. Wearily she struggled upright.

'What kind of a man are you?' she grumbled.

'I'm a man who offered you more money than you would ever have laid eyes on,' he reminded her. 'But you don't get it laying around in bed.'

'All right.'

'Your clothes are on that chair,' he pointed.

'Yes, yes.'

She got up and paddled over to the chair. There was scarcely enough daylight to see properly. What kind of time was this? It must be before six in the morning.

'Whassa time?' she yawned.

'Five-thirty,' he replied. 'Be downstairs in five minutes and you'll get coffee.'

Five-thirty. This guy had less emotion than a fish. How could he be up and doing at this hour? Especially when you thought about everything. Still. She grinned quietly to herself. He wouldn't fool her again, not entirely. There was more to Benedict than the grim, efficient machine she'd been with the last few days. Much more. Come to think of it, there was more to him than most of the guys she'd ever known. She picked absently at the stuff on the chair. What was this? And this? Must be some kind of gag.

Benedict sat in the kitchen smoking. He'd finished one cup of coffee, and the cigarette was hitting the spot. This was the day. Everything that could be planned ahead had been done. There was no more fussing about details now. Now you played it as it came. There would be the unforeseen, the unplannable, there always was. Careful thinking ahead could reduce these risks, to a minimum, but not below a certain point. When they happened, that was when you could distinguish the thinkers, the professionals. He felt relaxed and comfortable. He always did when the time got near, confident that there was nothing forgotten, nothing overlooked. The girl had helped. She'd been good, and a welcome relief from weeks of worrying.

'Hey, what is this, some kind of joke?'

Toni's irritable voice from the door made him look up. She was wearing a faded black costume and thick heavy shoes. They struck a discordant note against the attractive angry face with the golden hair tumbled anyhow.

'No joke,' he replied. 'Get some coffee and sit down.'

Muttering to herself she poured a cup of the steaming liquid and sat opposite him.

'I can't figure you,' she grumbled. 'All that trouble you made me take to buy nice things, then you put me in this outfit.'

'You'll wear it four or at most five hours,' he informed her. 'Then you ought to draw ten thousand dollars. That's two thousand dollars an hour. So what's the beef?'

It was something to do with the job. Well, at least it wasn't some weird joke. Mollified, she sipped at the coffee. It was good. Benedict said nothing. He pushed cigarettes towards her and she lit one. Already she was feeling better. Better enough to think back to the night. Her eyes softened as she looked at the enigmatic figure opposite. What was it with him?

'Did you ever shoot a gun?' he asked, cutting in on her thoughts.

'No. I used to carry one around one time. But I never fired it.'

He put his hand in his pocket and slid something across the table. When he took his hand away there was a small pearl-handled automatic resting there. She stared at it with fascination.

'Wh-what's that for?' she stammered.

'That's for you, baby. In case you might want to shoot somebody. Pick it up, it won't hurt you.'

Gingerly she did as she was told. It wasn't heavy. The safety catch would be this doodad on the side. She clicked it down. Benedict nodded.

'Good, you seem to know what that's for. The rest is easy. C'm on in the other room. We got some rehearsing to do.'

The gun still in her hand, she followed him out.

* * *

There was a noise outside somewhere. Tip woke quickly, trying to identify the sound. Then he rolled off the couch and tiptoed to the door. As he reached it, it opened and Jerry stared at him.

'What are you gumshoeing around for?' demanded the newcomer.

'Heard a noise,' explained Tip.

'Oh. That was me. Some stuff to carry in. Come give a hand.'

Tip resented his tone, but wasn't awake enough to argue. He followed the stocky man down the wooden steps and across to a blue convertible. He hadn't seen this one before. It hadn't been there when they arrived last night. Jerry opened the rear door. Tip stared.

'What is it, a fancy dress party?'

'Never mind that. Just help carry it.'

He shrugged and grabbed an armful. A few minutes later it was piled on the floor in the rear room. An idea was beginning to take shape in Tip's mind. He was just about to put it to Jerry when he remembered they weren't supposed to talk. He checked his watch and saw it was six o'clock.

'What do we do next?' he asked.

'We wait,' Jerry informed him.

'How long?'

Jerry looked at him, and the look was not friendly.

'I don't know how long,' he said slowly. 'We get told to wait, we wait. Maybe an hour, maybe all day. We do like he says. One thing you got to learn in this business, is do what you're told.'

'All right. So we wait.'

'I'll get coffee in a little while,' promised Jerry.

★   ★   ★

Somebody was banging on that damned door again, Gorman swore and threw a heavy boot at it. On the other side somebody laughed.

'Six o'clock, Mr. Gorman. You said to wake you at six.'

He groaned. He didn't know why he bothered to go to bed at all. Then he remembered something.

'Get in here a minute,' he roared.

The door opened and a laughing youngster came in.

'If you have to drag a man out of bed when he's had no sleep, at least have the decency not to laugh at him.'

'Sure thing, Mr. Gorman.' The boy was still smiling widely. 'Something I can do for you?'

'Yeah. You know that little creep Bushman took off last night?'

'Yessir.'

'Do we know if he stole anything?'

'Could have. I hear somebody bust the lock on the costumes wagon last night. That could have been Bushman.'

Gorman scratched at the stubble on his chin. 'Could be,' he mused. 'Any stuff gone?'

'Gee, Mr. Gorman, I don't know. There's hundreds of costumes in there. It would take hours to check 'em all. You want it done?'

Hours. The boy was right. It *would* take hours. And all they'd know at the end of it was whether or not a few lousy costumes were missing. And today of all days there just wasn't that much time.

'No,' he decided. 'We have enough to do without that. I'll get to it later. Well, you know what day it is?'

'Sure do, Mr. Gorman,' grinned the boy. 'We're going to wake up that town with the greatest old parade they ever did see.'

'Not if everybody's like you, standing around chewing the fat while there's work waiting. Don't let me keep you.'

'No, sir.'

The door slammed behind the fleeing youth. Gorman chuckled. That was a good kid that one. He was circus. Not like that little runt Bushman. Why would he want to steal costumes? Come to that, had he really taken anything at all? Well, there was plenty to do around here without wasting valuable time on him.

Gorman stumped to the door and flung it wide.

'Coffee,' he bellowed.

*   *   *

Bushman whistled blithely as the ancient car bounced and rattled its way along the highway. This was living. Beyond any shadow of a doubt, this was living. A wide open road, no ties, and a pocket full of money. Plus a feeling he'd done something. All his life he'd wondered what he'd do if a real big opportunity came his way. Well it had. And what did he do? Why, he grabbed it with both hands, that's what. And now he was free and clear as a bird. He was glad about that, glad there'd be no more contact with guys like that. The warm morning sun was heating up the air fast, but he felt a sudden shiver at the memory of those cold, hard men. The big feller, he was the worst. Or was he? That other one, the one with the knife, he'd been a real bad one too. Yep, he was lucky to be rid of both of them. And what could they possibly want with that stuff? They could have bought the whole lot, legit, for a lot less than they paid him to steal it. It didn't make any kind of sense. Still that wasn't his worry. He didn't have any worry.

The jalopy coughed and almost bounced him off the seat. One more protesting splutter, and the motor died. He cursed and got out. It wasn't any use raising the hood. What went on under there was a total mystery to Bushman. He kicked at the fender and swore. A fine thing to happen. Before he'd had time to get really angry he saw a truck in the distance, coming towards him. A couple of minutes later, the big wagon pulled up beside him. A cheery red face stuck out of the window.

'Don't tell me that brand new Caddy broke down, pal?'

He nodded glumly.

'Any chance of a lift?'

The truckie looked him over carefully, decided he could handle any trouble Bushman might start.

'Sure. Hop in.'

Maybe it was for the best, the little man thought. This way, he was already rid of the car. As they bounced along, the driver asked:

'Which way you heading?'

'It doesn't matter.'

One of those.

'Say, if it didn't matter with me, I'd be going the other way.'

'Really? Why?'

'Pine Forks,' explained the driver. 'They are going to have the grandaddy of all wingdings in that town today and tomorrow.'

'Is that so? I hadn't heard about it.'

'That is so,' confirmed the driver. 'They even gonna have one of these real old-fashioned circus parades. Gonna be quite something. Sounds kinda corny I know, but I bet it's a lotta fun just the same. Yeah. The place to be today, friend, is Pine Forks.'

12

At eight-thirty Benedict called a halt.

'That's it,' he announced. 'I'm satisfied.'

Toni sighed with relief. She'd thought for the first hour she was going crazy. Then for another hour she'd gone on mechanically, moving without thinking, speaking her words and answering questions almost by reflex. The change had come at the beginning of the third hour. All at once, to the knowledge and the automatic responses was added something new. And the something was confidence. She could do it. No question phased her now, no twist in the conversation. She was equal to anything.

Benedict had sensed the moment at the same time as the girl, but he gave no sign. Instead he ground on remorselessly, prodding, trying to catch her out. But now he knew he was wasting his time. The girl wasn't going to be caught out, and that was fine. If he couldn't do it, with his carefully rehearsed questions, loaded with suspicion, the other guy wouldn't be able to either. And there'd be no suspicion in his mind in the first place.

Toni felt worn out, but triumphant. She'd done what he wanted, this human machine called Benedict. That meant he was satisfied, and if he was satisfied the operation had to work. Nobody could have worked so hard to find something wrong with her act, nobody could have been so suspicious and insulting. And it hadn't worked, not since she felt that moment when all came naturally.

'Go up and change your clothes,' Benedict ordered crisply. 'Those tight red pants you bought, what are those called?'

'Ballerina,' she told him.

'That's it,' he nodded. 'Put those on, and that black shirt thing with the white pockets.'

Toni didn't even object to being told what she should wear.

'Anything else?'

'Sure. Comb your hair out as much as you can. I want you so anybody sees you, he's going to remember a blonde with lots of colour on. Oh, and plenty of stuff on your face.'

Plenty of stuff on your face. Just like a man, she reflected. Upstairs she found the clothes he'd named and dressed swiftly. Then she put on too much make-up using the brightest lipstick she had. A few quick combs at the bright golden hair and she thought she would do. She scooped up the drab costume heavy shoes and the grey wig Benedict had made her wear. Tucking them all under her arm she went downstairs. Benedict looked at her critically.

'O.K.' he decided. 'Dump that in the case.'

There was a big brown case open on a table. Toni dropped the stuff inside. It didn't take up much room. The ancient purse went in too, with the little automatic inside.

'This thing will rattle,' she remarked.

'Only on the outward trip,' he said drily. 'Coming back it'll take a strong man to carry it.'

With mounting excitement, she realised

what he meant. It didn't seem possible they were really going to do what Benedict said. It all seemed unreal somehow, the kind of thing you talked about sometimes, half-joking, but not something you really did.

'Let's go.'

Benedict swung the case down into his hand and led the way out.

He drove carefully into town, noting the crowds beginning to gather in the streets. Toni thought everything fitted. It seemed right and proper there should be this air of expectancy in town, people out in a holiday mood. It showed something was going to happen. Something was, but not what these yokels imagined. What was Benedict up to now, was he crazy? He was driving straight towards a traffic police-man who was waving him down.

'Take it easy,' said Benedict softly. 'And be sure the guy gets a good look at you.'

He applied the brakes and stuck his head out of the window.

'What's the trouble, officer?' he asked in a mild tone.

The officer was about to reply when he

saw Toni's blonde head emerge from the other window. Then he swallowed the irritable words and smiled a wide smile.

'No trouble,' he assured them. 'Sorry to have to stop you, you too ma'am, but no traffic on Main today, on account of the parade.'

Toni gave him a brilliant smile. Suddenly it was worth while being on traffic duty in a crummy side street while all the people who didn't happen to be policemen were all set for a day's fun.

'But surely officer,' she wheedled, 'Nobody would mind just one little old car? We only want to watch the parade.'

The man on the other end of the smile grinned in a dazed fashion.

'Lady, believe me, it breaks my heart to refuse. But it's more than my badge is worth. Park the car and walk through a couple of blocks along.'

'Oh well, I'm sure you'd have helped if you could.'

She pulled her head in, and Benedict reversed the car around.

'Nice going,' he grunted. 'He won't forget you in a hurry.'

'The way he looked at me, he'll probably tear the town apart trying to find me when he gets off duty,' she chuckled.

Benedict drove expertly through the side roads. There was nobody around, either on the roads or walking. Pine Forks was going to see a parade. He pulled in outside what looked like a warehouse. Leaving the car, he took keys from his pocket and fitted one quickly. Then he pushed open the heavy wooden doors, came back and drove the car inside.

'Get changed. Here, in the car,' he told her.

Then he was gone, shutting the big doors before walking across to a flight of wooden steps at the far end of the place. Toni sighed and began to change her clothes in the cramped space available.

'Did you hear a car?' asked Tip.

Jerry nodded.

'It's O.K. It'll be him.'

'How d'you know it's him? Could be anybody, could be cops even.'

'Cool off. Nobody else but him has a key. And even if it was every cop in town, so what? We ain't doing nothing illegal.'

'Yeah.'

Just the same Tip kept straining his ears. The now-familiar squeaking of the wooden steps told him the new arrival was coming in. A moment later Benedict knocked at the door.

'It's me,' he announced.

Jerry grinned knowingly.

'C'mon, it ain't locked.'

The big man walked in, and nodded to them.

'Anything go wrong?'

He was talking to Jerry.

'Nah. The little guy turned up like you said. All the stuff is there.'

Benedict looked at the heap.

'You scare him away?'

'What's up, I'm an amateur or something? You said scare him, brother he's probably got white hair by now. But you'd have to go a long way to take a look at it.'

Tip listened carefully. That was where Jerry had gone during the night. To meet some character who'd given him the fancy clothes. And by the sound of it,

Jerry had knocked off the other man afterwards.

Benedict seemed satisfied.

'All right, it's today.'

'Ah.'

Both men said it at the same time.

'We don't have a lot of time, so I'll explain the whole deal to you while we get dressed.'

'It's as soon as that?' protested Jerry. 'Listen, I don't like the sound of it. A job needs time, lots of talk before you do it. I don't like to rush things.'

Benedict looked at him coldly.

'Nothing's being rushed,' he told him. 'Everything's being done the way I want it. The way I always work. Nobody ever had any complaints afterwards. You may think you're a mastermind, but to me you're just a cheap hoodlum who it so happens I can use this one time. You got anything to say, get it said. But remember this is my deal, and I'm not a three-time loser.'

Jerry breathed heavily. Tip watched with fascination. A three-strikes man, and right on the same job with him. He didn't know whether he liked the idea or not. A man with three penal terms behind him is due for life imprisonment next time he gets caught and convicted. So he doesn't get caught. He shoots first, because from where he stands he has nothing to lose. That meant if the going got rough, Jerry would be the best possible guy to have around, because he'd just stand there shooting back until he was dead. But suppose things weren't rough. Just suppose everything went like clockwork. This Jerry could gum up the whole deal. A guy in the spot he was in was just as likely to start blasting away every time a traffic cop held up a hand.

Jerry was staring at the floor now. The only sign of his agitation was the way he kept clenching and unclenching his thick hands. Well, that was a good sign anyway. The old guy knew how to control his temper. With people. Whether he could do the same thing with a badge remained to be seen.

'Is the big wagon out at the barn?' queried Benedict.

Jerry looked at him sourly.

'Natch. You said to put it in the barn, it's in the barn. Been there two days. And' he anticipated the question, 'It was still there two hours ago, because I checked.'

'O.K.' nodded the big man. 'I'll tell you this. That's just an extra comfort, that wagon. We can still do what we have to do whether it's there or not. But it'll be roses all the way if we have it.'

'You'll have it,' he was assured. 'And the car's all ready too. Say that was a swell idea you had about the car.'

'Did it once before,' grunted Benedict. 'Worked like a breeze, and the cops never did figure it. Let's get busy. The first thing is to get into these duds.'

They changed rapidly, checking each other's appearance at the end. When he was satisfied, Benedict said to Jerry:

'Go get the woman in here. We have a few things to straighten out on this deal before we move.'

Jerry nodded and went out to where Toni was.

'Boss says for you to come in now,' he told her.

Funny looking woman to be using on a

caper, he thought. Looked more like a middle-aged schoolmarm than anything else. Still, the big guy knew what he was doing, so she must be right for the job.

Toni nodded and got out, smoothing her clothes here and there as she stood upright. Only a man would expect a woman to be able to change clothes in a car. She wondered why this man with her was dressed up for a costume party, even to the plastic face. Well, it was a fair exchange she decided. He wasn't seeing what she looked like either, not what she really looked like.

Inside, Benedict had cleared a table, and now stood waiting, a stick of chalk in his hand. When Toni and Jerry arrived, he said:

'O.K., we'll take this from the top. Everything is quick and easy, and if we have to, we've got time to go through it twenty times. So don't worry if you don't get the whole pitch the first time round. All set?'

They all crowded round the table. Benedict began to draw, then he chuckled.

'I just thought of something. We're probably going to be seen by more eye-witnesses than anybody in history. Here's what I mean.'

As the chalk moved, his voice droned on.

13

The West Coast Mutual Farmers Bank stood on the corner of Main and Pine Street. Square in the centre of town, it was one of the oldest buildings. First there was the saloon and hotel, then a general trading store. Next came the sheriff's office and jail, then the express office. The bank followed within a few years, and was now a building to point out with some pride, a link with the old west. Not that Arnold Carmody, the president, was keen on the association of ideas.

'A bank has to be two things,' he was fond of saying. 'It has to be the symbol of four-square respectability and decency. And at the same time it must be progressive in its outlook, in touch with modern developments.'

The W.C.M.F. was usually in the forefront of modern business thinking, always alive to the markets, business trends and so forth. Old man Carmody had created a living monument to his far-sightedness over a span of fifty competitive years. Land development, moving pictures, munitions. A condensation of the bank's trading record for half-a-century read like a potted history of the progress of American finance.

The first small bank to be fitted with anti-robbery devices. Carmody had been alive to the ever-present threat of the bank raider. Long before most bankers had been forced into it, Carmody had installed the latest most expensive equipment to foil possible raiders. When the other small men in many parts of the country were being terrorised in the twenties and thirties, the W.C.M.F. had remained untouched. In Pine Forks there was a saying. If your money's in Carmody's bag, it's safer than at Fort Knox.

And so the legend grew. Attempts had been made at different times to test the devices Carmody had installed. All had failed, and the legend gained more ground. But despite his dynamic approach, there was no gainsaying the fact that Carmody was no longer young. Approaching his seventy-sixth year, he tended to linger more on the glories of the past, and pay less attention to the present, hardly any at all to the future. A particularly tender spot was the bank's security system.

'What's wrong with it?' he would snap.

'Well, sir, nothing. Nothing at all. The truth is, that system was installed in nineteen twenty six, and there have been great advances in the field since that time.'

'Been a lot of banks robbed, too,' he would snort. 'You won't find the W.C.M.F. on the list.'

'No, sir, the system has proved its worth, no doubt of that. It's just that almost forty years have passed, and we ought to get up with the times.'

'Rubbish. Had it brought up to date in nineteen forty — forty — '

'Forty four, sir.'

'Exactly. In nineteen forty four. And that commission of inspectors from the Central Banks Council in the following

237

year. You know what they gave me? Well, do you?'

'Yessir. A certificate.'

'Damn right. A certificate. It said the old W.C.M.F. could hold its own with the best. Could then and it can now. I don't blame you for trying though. Wouldn't hire you if you didn't have ideas. You have to learn to distinguish between improving things and just changing things. They don't always go hand in hand. That system is the best, and only a fool tries to improve on that.'

Old man Carmody wasn't at the bank today. He had a grandstand view of the town centre from a room at the Alphonse Hotel across the street. He and a few other leading town dignitaries. It was a relief to the manager Walt Penrose. It was always a relief not to have the irascible president breathing down his neck all the time. You'd think after twenty years loyal service a man could be trusted with just a little authority sometimes. But it was only on rare occasions such as today that Penrose could really feel himself to be managing anything. The old man hadn't always been so authoritarian, but that business with Hacker had shattered his trust considerably. It wasn't surprising really. And old Carmody had put a lot of faith in Hacker and his ability. Then after eight years of hard work and steady promotion, Hacker had walked off with fourteen thousand dollars in cash. It had been a great blow to the old man's pride. It had been he, Penrose, who discovered the defalcation, and conveyed the news personally to the president, not breathing a word to any other member of the staff. It had turned out to be the smartest thing he ever did. Carmody swore him to silence, and made good the money from his own pocket. The very next day Penrose had been made manager, with a substantial raise in salary. That had been over four years ago, and the secret of Hacker's sudden departure had remained between himself and the old man ever since.

It had been a busy week for the W.C.M.F. People had been pouring into town from outlying districts for the centenary celebrations. The two-day wingding was putting happy smiles on a lot of faces around town, particularly on those belonging to store owners. Everyone was using the trip as part-business and part-pleasure, a thought which had occurred to the City Council when they agreed to devote substantial public funds to the celebrations. With many places of business being closed for the day, people seemed to be spending with a frenzied determination. All week there had been small queues of cheerful proprietors of small businesses, depositing the swollen takings from the merrymakers. A man wouldn't imagine there could be much money left in the town to spend on the official celebrations, which weren't due to start until today. But Penrose knew from long experience that if it's needed for reasons of personal relaxation, the money always seems to be available somehow. Tomorrow morning, they would be back, the happy depositors.

On Pine Street a middle-aged woman in a rusty black costume picked her way apologetically through the thickening crowds. She looked out of place among the gay shirts of the men and the bright dresses of the women. Up by the corner, where the view of the parade would be best, the people were standing close together and here she had difficulty in getting through.

'No use shoving, lady, we been waiting here close on an hour. You shoulda come early.'

A big man looked round at her, refusing to budge. Her lip trembled.

'But I have to get into the bank.'

'Oh.'

Turning, he pushed an authoritative arm into the crowd.

'Make way, there; this lady has to get to the bank.'

They weren't eager, but they grudgingly gave enough ground to let the woman through. One or two of the women looked with sympathy at the faded clothes and the grey hair.

Finally she emerged into the ten-foot gap which had been kept clear for access to the bank.

The three cowboys who appeared on Main Street attracted much amusement.

They looked like the real thing, with their worn check shirts and stained pants. Calf length boots were scuffed and cracked, and the aged stetson hats had seen a lot of weather. Only the gunbelts seemed new, they and the gleaming silver forty-fours which swung easily at their hips. Their faces were familiar too, John Wayne, Gregory Peck, James Stewart. Although Peck and Stewart were each about four inches shorter than they had any right to be.

'Hey, Greg, how 'bout a date tonight, behind the barn?' trilled a teenage girl.

'You wanta watch out you don't shrink up like them other fellers Mr. Wayne.'

'Say, where'd you guys leave Bronco Lane?'

The cowboys waved and laughed, handing out leaflets to anybody who would take one. The slips announced that the Gorman Brothers Grand Circus would definitely present the greatest show Pine Forks had ever seen. As they reached each store entrance they all trooped inside, bidding every one good morning and distributing the bright coloured papers. Pat Gorman stood up in his stirrups and looked behind him. The big chestnut mare snickered softly and pawed delicately at the ground. She was aware this was a special occasion. It was only on such occasions that the heavy man with the loud rough voice and the gentle hands climbed on her back.

'Get in line there,' bawled Gorman. 'We got a parade to put on here.'

All along the line people waved and smiled to show they were ready. Gorman snorted and leaned down to the silent figure beside him.

'Hey Ed,' he whispered hoarsely, 'You sure about those 'roos? Be a hell of a note if those beasts started jumping into the crowd or something.'

The big man nodded reassuringly.

'It's O.K., Pat. I told you twenty times already. Those animals were in a parade down Broadway, New York City, just last year. If they didn't act up then, they're not going to get excited over a few thousand people in Pine.'

Gorman nodded in return. He was sure Ed was right. Ed was always right about things like that. He looked at his watch again.

'And where's Rajah?' he shouted. 'What's the matter, I haven't got enough to do around here, I have to dress the elephants too?'

'He's coming.' Ed pointed.

The huge ponderous figure of Rajah appeared, a rolling grey mountain of hide, with a scarlet blanket over his back and a headdress sparkling with a thousand pieces of coloured glass. On his head sat Princess Jiva, dark and Eastern, her face composed in its habitual imperious mask.

Gorman watched as she swayed impassively towards him, the sun winking from the blood-red ruby stuck in the centre of her forehead.

'I'm always telling you, Nellie,' he grumbled. 'You'll cut it too fine one of these days.'

'Ole Raj and me never missed a parade since we started working together, Mr. Gorman. And you've never known us late either.'

There wasn't much of the Taj Mahal in the strident voice. With no more ado, the princess rolled by and took up a position ten yards ahead of Gorman. The circus owner took a last look at his watch.

'Start the music,' he ordered.

A stirring march crashed out from the leading wagon, and Gorman waved his top hat from side to side. The princess whispered to Rajah who immediately began his stately march forward. Gorman winked at Ed, who smiled and winked back.

'Best damn parade they've ever seen down here, Ed,' beamed Gorman.

'See you the other side of town in about an hour.'

'Knock their eyes out, Pat,' encouraged the other.

In the West Coast Mutual Farmers Bank, a man stood by the door peering out.

'No sign yet,' he reported.

The two leaning on the counter both grimaced.

'You better get back, Mr. Dooland,' said the woman in the green costume. 'You know what Mr. Penrose said about the staff peeking.'

Dooland sighed and joined the others.

'It's ridiculous,' he fretted. 'One day in one hundred years. You'd think they could have let us have just the morning free.'

The others nodded in silent agreement. The other man, a tall spare figure in his late twenties, stroked his chin the way old man Carmody always did.

'Let me tell you something, Dooland,' he mimicked. 'The W.C.M.F. never closed its doors once, not one time, in fifty years. 'Cept Sundays that is. And it isn't going to start now. And for what? A declaration of war? A visit from the President of the United States? No. A circus parade, Dooland. A march past of half-starved animals. No sir, I do not see my way clear to shutting down the business of the West Coast Mutual Farmers Bank, for the sake of a pack of bareback riders and clowns.'

The woman poked a sharp forefinger into the speaker's ribs.

'Ouch.'

'All I have to say, Mr. Carmody, is this,' she informed him. 'If the spectacle is so degrading, why is it all right for you to book yourself a grandstand view from the Alphonse?'

Both men muttered their agreement.

'If we were working, if there was any business,' grumbled Dooland. 'I wouldn't mind. That I could understand. But we haven't seen a customer all morning, and we all know perfectly well we're not going to until this parade is past and gone.'

Through the glass doors the younger man saw a grey-haired woman approaching.

'Bet a dollar you're wrong, Dooland,' he said quickly.

'You have a bet, Rogers,' chuckled the other.

The door opened and a figure in a crumpled black costume came slowly in. The woman clerk chuckled softly and Dooland swore under his breath. All three bent their heads as though deep in the bank's affairs. The newcomer peered uncertainly from one to the other. Then, as though having considered each of them carefully, she walked up to Rogers cubicle. He looked up with a professional smile.

'Can I help you, madam?'

The parade was into Main now, and the crowd had entered into the spirit of it. So what if it was corny? It was a parade, wasn't it? And nothing more interesting had happened around Pine Forks in a long time. The older people stirred with memories as the jangling music hit the still air and the colourful figures of the performers moved slowly past.

'Hey, lookit the kangaroos.'

'Boy, I wouldn't let one of them brutes come at me that way, gloves or no gloves.'

'Bert, I suppose there can't be any danger from those lions? I mean, those locks on there look sort of flimsy to me.'

In front, the Princess Jiva sat calmly on the elephant's massive head. Say, this really was quite a parade after all. Just like the folks used to talk about. The way it was in the old days. Seemed like a nice little town. That bunch of old goats up there on the balcony, they must be the town elders or something.

The circus master rode splendidly down the centre of the street, raising the shining silk hat in an occasional gesture, like some visiting royal personage.

The three cowboys stood inside Schultz's Hardware and watched Gorman pass.

'Give him another fifty yards,' whispered the one with the John Wayne face. 'He may look round.'

Rogers waited for the woman to speak. She seemed nervous.

'I wanted to talk to somebody about George Hacker.'

The young man didn't know what she was talking about. Still looking polite, he said in a puzzled voice.

'George Hacker, ma'am? Would Mr. Hacker be one of our depositors?'

Dooland pricked up his ears. Then he walked along behind the counter to stand beside Rogers.

'I beg your pardon, madam,' he smiled. 'But did I hear you mention George Hacker?'

She nodded, pleased.

'Why, yes, do you know him?'

'Well, I certainly did know him,' he admitted. 'George has not been with us for some years.'

Turning to Rogers, he said:

'Shall I attend this lady, Mr. Rogers? The man she's asking about, Mr. Hacker, was a colleague of mine here some time back. Before you joined us.'

'Why, of course, Mr. Dooland,' Rogers moved back. 'Ma'am.'

Dooland stared at the woman with more than polite interest. He had always been firmly convinced there was something very wrong about the way George Hacker suddenly disappeared like that. No notice, no message, nothing. And to make it even more curious, Penrose had been promoted right after it happened. Natural interest among the staff had been quickly stifled. Everyone was given to understand in no uncertain manner that George Hacker was not to be a subject for speculation, nor for that matter, ordinary conversation. These restrictions quickly had their effect and before long his name was never mentioned. Of the staff in those times only two remained, Dooland and Penrose himself. Why, he hadn't given Hacker more than a passing thought in years. And now, from the blue, here was this woman talking about him.

'You were saying something about George Hacker, ma'am? By the way my name is Dooland.'

'Oh yes, Mr. Dooland, thank you. I'm Amy Hacker, George's wife.'

Wife. Dooland licked his lips with nervous excitement. This was going to be more than casually interesting. Hacker never mentioned any wife.

'Anything I can do for you, Mrs. Hacker, will be a pleasure. But perhaps you'd like to tell me about it.'

'Well — ,' the woman hesitated and looked at the others, still busy looking busy. 'Is there a private office perhaps where we could talk? This is very public here isn't it?'

Dooland was disappointed. There was a private office. To be accurate, there were two. One was that of the president himself, where no one would ever dare enter. The other belonged to Penrose, and though in the ordinary way Dooland would have had no hesitation in borrowing the room under the circumstances he would need to explain to the manager why he needed the room. And he knew that once Hacker's name was mentioned, Penrose would take over personally. Perhaps he could persuade her to change her mind.

'I'm terribly sorry, Mrs. Hacker, but the private offices are in use at the moment. I can give you my personal assurance that everyone behind this counter has the complete trust of the bank president himself. Your confidence will be entirely respected.'

She nodded uncertainly.

'I'm sure of that, Mr. Dooland. But this is so terribly confidential.' Leaning forward, she beckoned Dooland. He lowered his head until their faces were no more than inches apart. 'It has to do with a police matter. I don't know whether this bank may be involved.'

'Involved?' The puzzlement in his voice was not assumed. 'The W.C.M.F. involved? I don't think I quite follow, ma'am. George left here years ago.'

'Oh yes, so I learned. But it seems these — these terrible things they accuse him of, they've been going on for years too. You mean the police haven't been here to see you yet?'

Dooland thought fast. Police business put a different complexion on this entirely. He'd been hoping for a cosy little talk that might produce some juicy information about Hacker. Police. He shuddered inwardly. The thought of any police matter involving the West Coast Mutual Farmers Bank was too rich for Dooland's blood. This was over his head. Curiosity was one thing, and nobody would blame him too much for that. Stupidity was something else again, particularly the kind which would involve withholding this kind of thing from the proper authorities. Reluctantly he suggested:

'I think you really should discuss this with our manager, Mr. Penrose, ma'am. A matter involving the bank such as you imply, ought really to be dealt with by him. Please excuse me.'

He went to the door marked 'Manager' and tapped on it.

'Who is it?'

Penrose's irritable voice came through

the door. He wasn't really annoyed about anything. Ordinarily he was a man of equable temperament, and on the best of terms with everyone. But ordinarily, the fire-eating Carmody was in the next office. It was one of those little human failings on Walt Penrose's part, that when the explosive president was absent he assumed a touchy manner himself.

Dooland opened the door and slipped inside, closing it behind him.

'Walt, there's a lady outside I think you ought to see yourself.'

'Oh?' Penrose looked surprised. 'Something you can't handle?'

Dooland flushed slightly.

'Let's say it's something I think you'd prefer me not to handle. She's George Hacker's wife.'

Penrose stared in amazement and rose slowly to his feet.

'She's what?'

The teller repeated what he'd said.

'His wife?' echoed the manager. 'But how can that be? I mean, I never heard Hacker was married, did you?'

'No, I didn't,' admitted Dooland. Then

he couldn't resist adding, 'But then, I never heard why he left so suddenly either. And this woman, she says she's here because of some crimes George is accused of. By the police.'

He savoured the last words, knowing the kind of shocked reaction they would produce. He wasn't disappointed.

'Police,' muttered Penrose.

In the bank, the sound of the excited crowds outside came through clearly. The two tellers and Mrs. Hacker stared through the doors at the massive figure of Rajah the elephant as he clumped heedlessly down the centre of Main Street. He didn't care about the crowds, the noise, or even the hot sun. All he cared about was the soft voice of the dark woman who was sitting on his neck, and the tidbits he knew would be forthcoming when all this walking was done.

'Boy oh boy, get a load of that dame on the elephant.'

'Poor beast, he's probably treated with the most awful cruelty. T'isn't natural for a dumb creature to be all dressed up like that.'

255

'Say, if those stones are real, they must be worth a fortune.'

'I'll bet that ringmaster's sweating in that outfit.'

Pat Gorman replaced the topper firmly on his head as he passed the West Coast Mutual Farmers Bank. He didn't know he was passing it, in fact he'd never heard of the W.C.M.F.

On the balcony of the Alphonse Hotel, Arnold Carmody spoke to the nervous little man beside him operating a camera.

'You're getting all this, I hope?'

'Yessir, Mr. Carmody, every foot of it.'

'H'm.'

The old man was pleased. For some time he'd been thinking of making a film about the W.C.M.F. The trouble was, a film is not like a book. With a film you have to have movement if you're going to sustain the interest. And now, heaven sent, was this glorious free spectacle passing right in front of the door. He hadn't worked out in detail just how it would fit into the film, but the important thing at the moment was not to miss this once in a lifetime opportunity.

On the other side of the street three cowboys inched their way through the crowds, handing out leaflets.

'Where's your horse, mister?'

'You guys are heading the wrong way. Hollywood's that-a-way.'

The tallest one, the one with the plastic John Wayne mask, laughed and joked with the crowd as they moved through.

Penrose was worried. It would be his rotten luck to have this woman call when Carmody was not available. Right this minute he could go to the entrance and see the president across the street, even wave at him. But he might as well be in China. Nobody could cross through that circus parade. Still, it wouldn't last for ever. Fifteen minutes, maybe twenty. The thing to do was get the woman comfortable and keep her talking until Carmody could be sent for.

'All right, bring her in. And see to it we're not disturbed.'

Dooland went back outside and raised the flap of the counter.

'If you'll please come through, Mrs.

Hacker, Mr. Penrose will be pleased to see you.'

'Thank you.'

She walked unhurriedly through the gap and to the open door. Penrose stood waiting for her.

'Please come in, won't you, and have a seat?'

He closed the door carefully.

Outside the other two looked enquiringly at Dooland, but he said nothing. The last time George Hacker had been a topic of conversation Penrose had had a promotion. Maybe this time, if he didn't put a foot wrong, there would be something he could turn to his own advantage.

The cowboys reached the open strip between the crowds leading to the bank entrance.

'Remember,' whispered the tall one crisply, 'Keep your fingers off those triggers unless I start shooting.'

Passing out their coloured notices on either side they walked into the bank. Nobody gave them a glance once they had passed. Who wanted to look at a bunch of imitation cowboys while there were cages of big cats passing? Lions, tigers, leopards, this was the stuff to watch.

The staff watched the cowboys come in. Well at least they were going to get some circus. The tall one put his hand inside his shirt and threw a cloth bag on the counter. Printed in large letters on the outside were the words 'STOLEN LOOT'.

'This is a stick-up,' he announced. 'Fill up the bags.'

The other two men tossed over similar bags. The tellers laughed.

'What time is the show, fellers?'

The one with the Gregory Peck mask drew his gun and pointed it.

'The show is on,' he said harshly. 'Fill up the bags.'

Dooland laughed rather nervously.

'Come on, now,' he said, 'It's a joke isn't it?'

'Sure. You ever tried laughing with a bullet in your belly? Snap it up.'

The other two men drew their shining silver guns from their holsters.

The woman teller turned a sallow colour. Dooland nodded.

'Do as he says.'

He picked up the nearest bag and began to push bundles of bills inside. At the same time he moved a switch with his right foot. Beads of sweat ran down his cheeks from fear as he did it. In Penrose's office a red light suddenly flashed on the wall over the door. It took about one second to register. A hold-up? Long training told in the emergency. There was no time for thinking, only action. The keys of the main safe lay in his desk drawer. All he had to do was take them out, drop them into the steel chute beside the desk and the bulk of the bank money would be safe. The light would flash for only ten seconds. At the end of that time, if he hadn't broken the connection, steel shutters would fall into place over every window and door. The mouth of the steel chute would be sealed electrically and nobody could get in or out of the place. Ten seconds.

Automatically he slid open the drawer and took out the keys. He'd forgotten his visitor in the emergency.

'Hold it. Press the button.'

He looked up then, alarmed by the sudden change in her tone. His heart jumped at the sight of the weapon pointing at him. Still he could not comprehend that this mousey woman was holding a gun.

'Switch off,' she screamed.

The tight skin on her knuckle gleamed suddenly white as her finger hardened on the trigger. Penrose knew he was staring at death. His hand moved quickly to the button on the underside of the desk and the flashing light ceased.

Mrs. Hacker relaxed. Her mind was filled with a jumble of conflicting thoughts at that moment. But dominant among them was the awful knowledge, the certainty that she would have squeezed the trigger if this frightened man hadn't done as he was told.

The door behind opened and the tall bandit came in.

'All right you,' he snapped. 'Open the safe.'

The keys jangled metallically as Penrose took them in shaking fingers.

'Listen,' the big man held a cold gun barrel against his ear, 'If we get caught, everybody dies. Everybody. Just move fast. You' to the woman 'Get out front and watch the doors.'

Outside, the noise of the parade was building up to a crescendo. Camels stomped delicately along, turbaned harem girls aboard, and a van supplying shrill Eastern music in the centre. Some way behind, the rival blare of powerful military band music followed the prancing aristocrats of horseflesh, the trick riders.

Penrose worked quickly, pulling bills from the shelves and dropping them into the waiting bag. The sound of marching music grew louder. The tall man with the gun said:

'That's enough. Outside.'

Penrose didn't quite understand. There was still a great deal of money left in the safe. This man couldn't seriously intend not to take it all.

The frightened manager scuttled through the door as fast as he could.

The woman was by the door looking

out. The other two men were holding their bulging bags with the ridiculous inscriptions. They all watched the big man.

'All right, in front of the counter, all of you.'

The staff moved hesitantly to the indicated spot. The female teller was almost unconscious from fear and shock, and Dooland had to keep his arm round her to support her.

'Smart,' approved the leader. 'You're being smart. Nobody's going to get hurt if you keep it that way. You two — '

The other men looked at him expectantly.

' — cover these heroes. If anyone moves, kill him.'

They planted themselves square in front of the counter, while the big man moved to the window and stared out.

There were twenty-four of the high-stepping circus horses, and the leading two were almost parallel with the windows. The gaily-painted van was half-way down the street, music emanating raucously from six speakers. People in its direct path held hands to their ears as it passed. The leader watched carefully, noting the snails-pace progress of the motorised van.

Now. He walked unhurriedly behind the counter and found the switch Dooland had operated. Carefully he clicked it into position. Through the open door of Penrose's office he could see the flashing red light. Ten.

'Get to the door,' he commanded, swinging his bag to one shoulder. The two men moved back slowly, not taking their eyes from the row of frightened tellers.

Seven.

'You're lucky I didn't kill you for switching that alarm.'

Dooland blanched as the big man addressed him softly.

Four.

'Open the door and get out.'

The two men holstered their guns as the woman opened the door. Then all three walked out without glancing back.

The leader drew his second gun, pointed it at the floor and pulled the trigger twice. There were faint plopping noises and a cloud of grey gas began to rise.

The fifth pair of horses were jet-black, with silver tassels bobbing from their ears. The van was opposite the bank now, and the noise of the music at that range was deafening.

One.

The leader stepped quickly through the door pulling it behind him. Dooland let the woman slide to the floor as he jumped quickly forward through the choking gas. He was only two feet from the door when the steel grille slammed downwards. His eyes streaming he grabbed hopelessly at the metal rods, then buckled at the knees and collapsed.

Together, the cowboys walked through the crowd and down the side of the W.C.M.F. building into Pine Street. A few people watched them casually, noting the carelessly slung bags. Must have been some kind of fun on Main, these guys robbing a stagecoach or something. Like to have seen that. Still, maybe they do the stunt tonight at the show.

A hundred yards down Pine Street, a

red sedan was parked by the kerb. Several people noticed the cowboys climb in, followed by a middle-aged woman in a black suit.

The one in the Gregory Peck mask got behind the wheel.

'O.K. move out, and remember there's no hurry.'

The car eased forward. Inside four tense people watched in every direction for signs of pursuit. Nothing happened.

'All right, step it up, not too much.'

It was hot in the car. James Stewart put a hand up to his mask.

'Leave it where it is,' snarled the leader. 'We're not out of this yet.'

Gradually, the buildings thinned out and soon they were on the desert highway.

'Now you can go like hell,' came the instruction.

The driver nodded and put his foot down on the accelerator. In ten minutes, they were ten miles out of town. A large barn-like building came into view. The car stopped and the woman got out.

'Now remember, don't get excited.

Don't start shooting at anything that moves,' warned the big man. 'If there's anything unusual in there, come and tell me. I'll decide what we do. Got it?'

She nodded and walked across to the barn. The others watched anxiously up and down the road. The woman emerged again into the bright sunlight and waved.

'Phew,' muttered one.

'Get moving.'

The driver left his seat and quickly followed the way the woman had gone. A moment later there was the roar of a heavy engine and a big black removal van emerged from the barn, edging its way slowly to the road.

Good, good, thought the leader. This wouldn't be any time for a busted axle.

'All right give him a hand with those ramps,' he ordered.

The other man got out, and the leader slipped behind the wheel. From the barn, the woman appeared again, sweeping carefully with a yard broom along the path taken by the big van. As she reached the road, sweeping away all traces of tyre marks in the sand, the rear end of the sedan was just disappearing inside the van. As the remaining two men lifted the steel ramps and slid them inside she was busy again with the broom.

The truck-driver hopped into the van and began pulling off his clothes. In less than two minutes he was Jerry again.

'Let's see,' demanded the leader.

Jerry turned and looked at him.

'Too clean,' decided the other. 'Let's have a smear of grease somewhere and rub in a little dust. Then get this thing moving.'

'Kay.'

Jerry hopped down to the road as the woman came up carrying the broom. He was curious to know what she really looked like. All he'd seen was this old crone act. This Walker was smart all right. He even kept the boys and girls from getting to know each other. The woman waited to see if he was going to speak. He shrugged and went to the door of the truck and climbed in. Then he sat and waited for the signal.

The woman scrambled up into the interior, where the two men were waiting to close the doors. They clanged behind her with a hollow noise and for some reason they made her think of prison doors.

'All set?' asked the big man.

The others nodded and he banged hard twice with his hand on the metal doors. In the cab Jerry nodded to himself and started the huge vehicle forward.

The two men inside went to the far side of the car and began to change their clothes. The woman did the same, careful to keep the bulk of the sedan between them. Remembering her instructions she left her face until the end. She felt better, a whole lot better, in the black shirt-blouse with white edging, and the tight red pants. Despite the grim situation, she could hardly resist a grin at the thought of what she must look like, the young woman's body in the gay clothes and the head of a middle-aged woman above. Clothes changed, she slipped into the rear seat of the car and sat down.

Benedict peeled off the John Wayne face and saw with approval that Toni had followed orders.

'Hurry up,' he snapped.

Tip Brennan reluctantly put the comb back in his pocket.

'Fix that front number plate, I'll take the rear.'

Tools were ready, strapped to the inside of the hood. Tip began work on the plate. Toni wondered whether she could smoke. Her nerves were ragged, and it was an unnatural climax to the morning's events, this sitting calmly in a car with nothing to do.

'How's it coming?' called Benedict.

'Nearly through,' came the reply.

The false number plates had been screwed over the genuine ones. It was a simple job to remove them. Benedict opened the car door and tossed them inside. Toni watched without comment. Till now, she'd found there was always a good reason for anything Benedict did. It seemed almost disloyal to doubt him, but she felt the red sedan was a mistake. Number plates, well, anybody could fix those. It wouldn't do much good once a cop saw the rich red of the body, to pin any hopes in different number plates.

Cops weren't stupid. A car like this would shine like a beacon even in big-city traffic, leave alone a jerkville like Pine Forks.

'O.K. to smoke?' she asked.

Benedict looked at her swiftly.

'No. Definitely no smoking,' he ordered.

Thanks for being so polite about it. He'd be better occupied wondering how to hide a car this colour when they got back to town. What was he doing now? They were standing either side of the hood, him and the other guy, the young one.

'Now take it easy,' Benedict's voice reached her. 'If this stuff splits the deal will take twice as long.'

The other man nodded, and they both leaned over the front of the hood, hands down by the radiator. What were they doing there? Very slowly, their hands moved upwards, then back over the hood. A thin black line appeared, and they seemed to be — to be what? Rolling something?

Toni leaned forward in the seat to get a better view. Then she saw what the men were doing. They were rolling off the red paint. How do you roll off paint? No, wait. It wasn't paint at all. It was sheeting. Red plastic or rubber sheeting. The whole damned car must be covered in it. It wasn't a red car at all, it was black. No, not black. As more and more of the hood came into view she could see it was a deep blue colour.

Slowly, very slowly, the thin sausage of red film fattened as the men edged backwards. Toni sat back again. Why had she ever imagined this Benedict would pull a boner like that? Any ordinary Joe would have rushed the car to a garage and put a quick new spray over the original colour. And any cop with two cents worth of brains would be on the lookout for a new paint job. One scrape with a pocket knife and the original colour showed through. That would be an ordinary joe, not Benedict. He put the new colour on first, and not with a spray gun. The guy was a genius. They were finished at the hood now, and were working independently at the sides.

The big van lurched suddenly, twice.

The two men nearly lost their balance, and Toni slipped sideways on the seat. Damn fool driver, she thought.

Benedict got the signal. It meant they were within five miles of the town. He looked quickly at his own progress. Too slow, he wouldn't be ready in time. Neither would Brennan. With the flat of his hand he banged three times on the rear of the cab. Jerry slowed the van down to a crawl. There was the sudden wail of sirens in the distance.

Tip and the girl looked up quickly. Benedict stared back at each in turn.

'So it's cops,' he said evenly. 'Somebody just bust open a bank in town, you don't imagine the law boys are going to take the day off, do you?'

Tip looked longingly at the corner where the revolvers and gunbelts lay in an untidy heap. Benedict watched him.

'Get on with what you're doing,' he said harshly. 'This car can put you inside, kid. Those cops are not going to bother us.'

In front, Jerry listened to the growing sound of the sirens. There was no doubt they were heading towards him. Well, he'd been in plenty of spots like this before. But not for a long time, he remembered. The sun glinted suddenly on metal and the leading motorcycle roared into view. Bumping gently along, Jerry licked his suddenly dry lips.

There was a second machine behind the first. No more. Well, if things got rough, they could blast these two easy enough. Just the same, it would be better if they didn't have to.

The leading patrol officer swung in towards the van. Maybe this truckie would have seen something. He braked and got off the bike, raising a gauntleted arm to halt the oncoming van. Jerry braked gently and stuck his head out of the window. The second policeman now parked his machine next to the first and sat astride, waiting.

'Somepin' wrong, officer?' queried Jerry.

'Bank hold-up,' came the reply. 'You seen a red sedan full of cowboys go past?'

Jerry grinned in disbelief.

'Cowboys?' he repeated. 'What's it, April the foist?'

The officer scowled. He hadn't time to clown around with this idiot.

'Yes, cowboys,' he snapped. 'Did you see them?'

Jerry wiped off the grin. No point in making these guys mad. With a solemn face he said:

'No officer, I didn't see any cowboys.'

The second policeman snorted.

'We're wasting time, Kelly. These guys could be fifty miles upstate by this time.'

'Just the same they'd have had to pass this guy if they used this road,' returned his partner doggedly.

The second one called out:

'Did you see anything out at Prospector's Barn?'

Jerry shook his head.

'Didn't think to look,' he admitted. 'I ain't never seen anything there all the years I been passing. Why would I look now?'

To Kelly, the second policeman said, 'Those guys would see a big thing like this a way off. They'd know he wouldn't forget those costumes they're wearing. So what would you do?'

Kelly thought about it.

'I might just pull off the road, and get behind the barn long enough to let this thing go by.'

'Sure. Exactly. Let's go.'

They kicked on their starters, circled around the van, then with a wave to Jerry they went scorching up the road.

Inside, Benedict and the others listened with relief to the diminishing roar of the powerful motors.

'Phew,' said Tip.

'I told you not to worry,' replied Benedict. 'We're trying to get into town. They're only interested in people trying to get out. Now let's get the rest of this stuff off, and fast.'

Toni searched around for a handkerchief to wipe the perspiration from her face and hands. That had been a very bad moment for her. It hadn't been so much the prospect of discovery, even perhaps arrest that had frightened her. It had been the look on the young one's face as they crouched in the silent van. She had known what he would do if anyone had opened those rear doors. His eyes had flickered constantly to the guns, and he would not have hesitated to murder the unsuspecting policemen if there had been a risk of discovery.

Benedict too, had been watching Tip, but with a different reaction. His was one of approval. The kid wouldn't have held up his hands, and begged them not to hurt him. He was all set to shoot it out, and that was in his favour. The only thing that had worried Benedict was whether the strain of uncertainty might have proved too much for Brennan. Whether he might have just grabbed the nearest gun and started shooting when it wasn't necessary. But as it turned out, the kid was all right.

Three dull bangs announced that Jerry was moving again. Benedict and Tip were now at the rear of the sedan, unrolling the last of the red plastic film.

'Say,' breathed Tip admiringly. 'This was a great idea. Nobody, but nobody could ever tell this was the same car.'

Benedict looked at him coldly.

'You better pray you're right,' he advised. 'Once anybody ties this to the other car, we're dead.'

Talk of death prompted the younger man to ask a question.

'Er,' he began hesitantly, 'That gas. The stuff you dropped in the bank. Was that poison?'

'Would it make any difference?'

Tip shrugged with exaggerated nonchalance.

'No. Just wondered, that's all.'

'It wasn't poison. Make 'em sick for a few days. Nothing more. There wasn't any point in killing those people. They'll never be able to identify any of us.'

'Not us, no,' agreed Tip, 'But what about — ?' He jerked his head towards the car.

'Her least of all,' was the reply.

Inside the car, Toni was thinking about the driver, the man she'd seen for the first time back there in the road after he'd changed out of the cowboy clothes. He'd looked at her strangely, but that was probably no more than interest. After all, it was unusual to be working with somebody and never to get a good look at them. Not that his look had taught him much. He'd only seen the same face she'd had back at the bank, and her own face didn't look much like that. But she'd known him immediately. Older now, and with some of the insolence melted away from the lined face, there was no mistaking that the driver was Joseph Offerman. The man in the clipping she'd read from Benedict's wallet. That was a piece of information she possessed, and which even Benedict couldn't know she had. At that moment it seemed useless enough knowledge, but it was something. She felt secretly pleased to have this scrap of information. It changed the pattern just that little bit in a way that Benedict was less almighty. Till now, she'd felt that she and the others were like those little dolls on wires that the man operated. Puppets that's what they called them. That was it exactly. She and the other two men had been like puppets, with Benedict pulling the wires. Now there was something about her Benedict didn't know. And, not knowing, could not control. There was no reason to doubt the big man, and so far everything had gone the way he said it would. Just the same, she was just that little bit less helpless than before.

In front, the man who was unknowingly responsible for Toni's change of status drove steadily towards town. He'd handled those cops back there exactly right. Just like the old days, all the coolness returning at the right moment. There'd been a time, back there all those years ago, when that little run-in with the law would have been routine. When this Walker had dropped in out of the sky and calmly told him he was back in business, he'd had a few sleepless nights. For years now he'd done nothing more illegal than park his car on the wrong side of the street. And not from choice. He'd just got wise, that was all. With every law enforcement agency in three states looking for him he had a choice. He could either go on being the great Joe Offerman, knowing that in the end they would get him. If he didn't get killed he'd spend the rest of his life behind bars. Or he could quit. Quit cold, just drop right out of sight and be nobody. But a safe nobody. He'd got smart just in time. He looked for the right town, picked his moment, and suddenly there was no more Joe Offerman. Instead there was Jerry, the quiet little guy with the one-man trucking business. And it had worked. For the first few years he'd had a bad time every time he saw a uniform, but that had worn off gradually. For a long time now he'd begun to feel safe. Well, almost safe. A guy with a file as thick as that Offerman, he can never feel really safe. And he'd been right too. Because, like a visitor from another planet, this Walker had just strolled in one day and reminded him who he was. Before he had time to recover from the shock of that, Walker told him why he'd come. Either he could co-operate in this thing that was coming up, or he could wait for that knock on the door that would be the law.

Well, he never really had a chance. Anyway, there'd been a certain excitement in the prospect. Nobody likes to think he's getting old, and Jerry had felt this would be like the old days, when excitement was the daily ration. Just the same, he'd been relieved when that talk with the motor cycle cops had gone off so well. The bank raid, well that didn't really count. Anybody with Joe Offerman's record could hold a gun on a bunch of frightened nobodies. And use the gun if he had to. But the meeting with the cops had been a real test, something to be proud of. He shrugged from his mind the memory of his trembling hands as he watched the two motorcycles disappear up the road.

Now what? Up in front there seemed to be a jam of some kind, traffic pulled in to the side of the road. Police block. Then they were finished. There was no way out of this one, he thought desperately. If he turned this thing round, they'd be after him like a pack of wolves, with everything blasting. There was no other way than just to walk right into it. He hadn't got a gun. No gun. He didn't have a chance. Whatever got into that Walker, not to let him have a gun?

He was close now, and able to see what

was going on. There were two cop cars, the usual thing. They were parked crosswise to the road one either side and twenty feet apart. This meant the road was clear, but you had to slow down to ten miles an hour to get between them. A bunch of uniformed figures were facing the opposite direction, where a small line of cars waited. The two cops talking to the driver of the leading vehicle suddenly stepped away and waved it through. As the car passed him, Jerry could see the middle-aged couple in front arguing furiously.

Now. It was going to be now. One of the policemen was walking towards him. And he didn't even have a lousy gun. Those damned hands were shaking again. He knew he ought to say something but the words wouldn't come. Instead he sat staring grimly at the broad man who was pacing up to the van.

'Anything happening back up the road, man?'

The cop didn't sound suspicious, but friendly. That didn't mean a thing. The time you got to watch a copper is when he's friendly.

'Didn't see anything.'

Somehow the words croaked out from a dry throat.

'Oh?' the voice was hardening now. 'Thought you might have run across some of our boys.'

'Oh, them. Sure, I seen them. Wait a minute, Kelly was one. That right?'

Now he was friendly again.

'Sure, that's the pair.'

'Run into 'em a few miles back. Looking for some holdup guys. Asked me if they'd passed.'

'What did you say?'

'Nothing passed me. Kelly thought they could have got out of my sight behind the old Barn up there, then moved on again.'

'Yeah,' replied the policeman doubtfully. 'Yeah, that could be. Sorry about the delay. We're stopping everything trying to leave town.'

And now the confidence surged back.

'You're stopping everything trying to get in, too,' he pointed out. 'I have to get this stolen money back before noon, or they're going to charge interest.'

The cop grinned. 'O.K., but you know how it is. Wait while I back out of your way.'

'Thanks.'

Jerry relaxed behind the wheel while the hated uniform moved away. The officer got into the nearest car and reversed to the other side of the road. There was now a clear channel for the big van. He leaned out and waved. Jerry waved back and rolled slowly forward. Ahead, the little knot of policemen stepped aside and waved him on. Curious faces stared out of the cars waiting to clear the cordon, then they were behind him and he was through.

Less than five minutes later he swung into the side road that led to the rear entrance to the garage. Now he banged hard four times on the rear of the cab to let them know they'd arrived.

'What's that mean?' demanded Tip.

'It means we're almost there,' replied Benedict. 'All he has to do is open the doors and take this thing inside.'

'We made it,' exulted the younger man. 'We made it.'

Benedict shook his head.

'All we've done is get back where we started from,' he contradicted. 'We haven't made anything but a garage yet.'

Tip listened, but didn't take it in. They'd made it. This Benedict was too careful by half. Sure, you had to take it easy, cover your tracks and like that. But you didn't have to act like somebody's old maid aunt. What could go wrong now?

The van lurched, hesitated, then rolled forward a few yards. Either side of the sedan, the two men waited. Toni sat inside. She hadn't the vaguest idea where they were, and it was no time for her to be asking questions.

Jerry braked, looked around thankfully at the friendly safety of the garage. He got out and walked back to close the big doors. Then he thumped cheerfully on the van.

'Everybody out,' he called.

Benedict nodded, and he and Tip released the catches on the rear door of the van. He jumped down and looked into Jerry's grinning face.

'I'll say this for you man,' Jerry said 'You sure mapped out this beauty.'

'That's right,' agreed Tip.

'Plenty to do yet,' grunted Benedict. 'Including the toughest part, which is not to get feeling too cocky, for a long time.'

The others exchanged glances and winked.

'The dame too,' Jerry enthused. 'In the ordinary way I don't like working with dames, but that one was O.K.'

Benedict nodded and called over his shoulder.

'All right, in there. Let's go.'

Toni was waiting for him to speak. Now she opened the car door and climbed out, long slender legs tightening against the red ballerina pants. As she stood upright she was aware of Tip and the driver, the one-time Joe Offerman, looking at her. She remembered a conversation she once had with an ageing blonde hostess at about three a.m. one morning.

'Mob boys?' the blonde had said. 'You want to know about those guys, ask me. Ask Queenie. Listen I knew 'em all one time or another. They come in different sizes, according to the racket they're in.'

She'd continued with a lot of free information about the varying attitudes of racketeers towards women. According to Queenie, the attitude was determined by the particular nature of their calling. Toni was remembering what she'd said about hold-up men.

'Heisters? As for heisters, don't ask me. Please. Listen, those are almost the worst. Before a thing they're nervous, jumpy. They work up a steam over any little thing, and if there's a woman around, they can make life hell. And I don't mean the bed bit. That's out. But they can be plenty mean other ways. After the thing now, that's a different story. Then they unwind. They're all big important men then, and they want the whole world to know it. If there's a woman with them, she's the only little bit of world they have till the heat's off. So they have to show her. Don't ask me any more honey. I don't like to think back to those times. Just remember what I tell you. Any of those stick-up guys ever want you to throw in with 'em, the answer is no.'

Now, just ready to climb down, Toni was feeling the way the two men were eyeing her. They'd looked at her before, but this was more than looking. Considering the grey wig and the pencilled wrinkles on her face, she was thankful they weren't seeing her as she really was. Of course the younger one had had plenty of chances to look at her on the trip down. He knew what she really looked like. But Offerman, the one who called himself Jerry, he'd only seen her like this. And yet the look was still there, the look she would have expected after hearing the faded hostess on the subject. It was a good thing Benedict was around, she decided.

Benedict sensed the atmosphere at once.

'Let's get to work,' he said. 'The way we said. The blue sedan out of there first. And fast.'

Tip and Jerry got busy immediately. To Toni, Benedict said quietly.

'Go sit in the convertible and start cleaning up your face. Keep on the wig till I say off. I don't want these guys thinking about anything else but work.'

Toni turned to go, but Benedict put a hand on her arm.

'You still got the gun in your purse. If anything starts here, use it.'

She looked at him with worried eyes, then nodded and went to the car. What did he mean, if anything started? There was only one thing he could mean, and that was the money. If one of the others, or both of them, decided there was no need for so many to share in the profits, she was supposed to back Benedict. But would she? For that matter, did she want to? Then she thought of the way they'd looked at her, those others. Remembered too, the previous night with Benedict. Whatever the others had in mind, there were still two of them. If there was trouble she'd stand by Benedict. Unless, that was, he very obviously didn't stand a chance. That would be different. It was one thing to back him up for good reasons of her own. Quite another to stick out her neck for a lost cause. She would have to watch very closely. Very closely indeed.

Tip reversed the hold-up car very easily down the ramps. All this trouble seemed like a lot of unnecessary fooling around to him. They had the money. Why didn't they just split up and take off? This planning work and all that jazz, that was O.K. for getting the thing done. All right, so it got done. Why were they doing all this afterwards?

Jerry watched carefully as the sedan coasted smoothly to the garage floor. Whatever else you thought about the big guy, he certainly took no chances. Jerry had been around the rackets a long time before he went into voluntary retirement. One thing was for sure. The guys who made it big, they were the ones who worked it all out like this Walker. Jerry had a feeling, one he hadn't had in a long while. This was going to be all right. It was going to work out just the way Walker said. The only thing about which he felt uneasy was the shill. They always were a risk especially on a deal like this. In his younger days, he'd seen all kinds of trouble caused by dames like that. The wig didn't fool him. She may have the face of an old frump, but there was no mistaking the long legs and the rangy body. He'd seen dozens like her in the past, cool hard women who knew how to make a man's blood jump around. He was an old hand, a real pro. but just the same he'd felt that quick excitement for a moment a few minutes earlier. Felt the young punk's reaction too. Yeah, the woman could be the weak spot.

Benedict watched Tip drive the car to a parking bay then go back to give Jerry a hand replacing the ramps. As they went to close the big doors he called:

'Just a minute.'

Hopping up inside he went to the pile of costumes and began tossing them out. The other two gathered them up. Then, with a gunbelt in each hand and one over his shoulder, Benedict climbed down.

'Mustn't forget these, boys. Let's go get rid of 'em.'

Jerry moved to accompany him, but Tip stood firm.

'We're forgetting something else,' he said softly.

'Oh What's that' enquired Benedict mildly.

'The dough,' Tip reminded. 'It's over there in the sedan. The dame is sitting twenty yards from it. What are we gonna do? All walk away, and leave her to beat it with the whole take?'

Benedict listened gravely.

'How far do you think she'd get, carrying three heavy bags?'

'There's three cars here, she don't have to carry them at all.'

The big man nodded.

'Yes, there are three cars. You think she could drive one through those doors back there?'

Jerry held up a key for Tip to see, and grinned.

'Relax, kid, this ain't our first time out.'

Tip flushed. He didn't want anybody reminding him this was his first big job. A hunk of that dough was his. A big slice. He had a right to ask questions. These two guys seemed to think he was nobody. Well, they'd find out.

'Any more objections,' queried Benedict, and there was ice in his voice.

'No,' mumbled Tip.

Together the three men walked up the wooden steps, and into the rear room where Tip had spent the night. Jerry opened up the trap and dropped the clothes down the hole. The others did the same.

'What about the guns?' asked Jerry. 'They'd hang us as quick as the duds.'

'If anybody gets close enough to see them we'll need them.' Benedict replied flatly. 'We keep them while we're still using this place. Then we can dump them down there with the rest of the stuff.'

He handed a silver revolver to Tip, another to Jerry. Then he took one himself, and lowered the belts carefully down the hole. Tip checked the cartridge chamber quickly and found it was full. Jerry did the same, but not so quickly.

'Let's get those bags in here,' snapped Benedict.

Jerry shrugged and went out at once. Tip was sick of being ordered around now that the thing was done, but he caught the big man's cold gaze and went out too.

There'd been a shift in the atmosphere. A keen nose and ear for atmosphere had saved Benedict's life more than once, and didn't fail him now. As he left the room Jerry was coming back, toting a heavy bag.

Sitting in the convertible, Toni was busy wiping off her face with freshening pads. The wig was getting hot and uncomfortable and she'd have liked to pull it off and get a comb through her hair. But Benedict had said no, and that was that. Shifting the driving mirror, she wriggled around until she was satisfied, then began the painstaking job of bringing her face back to life. As she rummaged for eyeshadow, her fingers touched the uncompromising hardness of the small revolver. Fascinated she drew it out and stared at it. Would she really have killed that man at the bank? Shot him down, an innocent stranger? No, that couldn't have been right. She only thought she would, because she was all tensed-up and excited. In the silence of the car, she laughed at herself reassuringly. She could never have done such a thing if the chips had really been down. But the laugh had an unfamiliar hollowness.

The older man emerged and went across to pick up one of the bags. Then the young one, and after a pause came Benedict. As he turned and went back with the third bag, she watched him expectantly. She was hoping he'd signal her to follow, but there was no sign from him. Nor, for that matter, from the others. Why were they collecting the money, she wondered? Maybe something was wrong. Maybe she better get over there and find out what this was all about. No. Fear of Benedict kept her where she was. He'd said she was to stay there until he told her otherwise. She'd better listen, she decided.

In the outer office Jerry opened a deep drawer and took out a small portable radio. He carried it into the rear and began fiddling with the controls.

He was busy with his own thoughts. Thoughts about subtle changes in Tip

Brennan's attitude. Jerry had been all through the scene too often in the past. The man with the brains, the organisation, he was the guy to get it done. Everybody did as he was told, or they'd get somebody else. Because until the job was done, there was only one guy you couldn't do without, one guy you had to have, and that was mister brains. Afterwards, like now, was different. There was the dough, all safe and sound, and suddenly mister brains was just one more guy with a gun. No bigger, no better than anybody else. Just a man. That was the time insults were remembered, slights brought back to mind. It was the time too, when the genius character stopped shoving if he had any sense. The dumbest guy in the outfit could knock him off as easy as pie, and everybody else would mind their own business. Because in this game a man stood alone, once the need for organisation was past.

Tip came in and stood a second bag by the first.

'Radio, huh? Maybe we can pick up something about today.'

'There's a newscast almost due,' advised Jerry.

In the outer office Benedict heard the sudden loud music. Damn. A radio. There'd been none on view before and he hadn't counted on it.

The others did not look round as he came in. He dumped the bag and looked around till he saw what he wanted. A small square cushion. The music died away.

'Station 2 WBOL and your newscaster, Larry Baines.' The men tensed expectantly. Benedict walked over and picked up the cushion, then sat on a hard chair, tucking it beneath him.

'All state and county police authorities have set up emergency alert measures to trace the gang who today robbed the West Coast Mutual Farmers Bank here in Pine Forks this morning. We are asked to notify the listening public to watch for a red sedan which may carry three men and a woman. The men are dressed in cowboy clothes, stolen from Gorman Brothers Circus, and the woman is described as middle-aged, with grey hair. She is dressed in a black or dark blue two piece suit, and is of shabby appearance.'

Tip snorted with derision and met black looks from the others.

'For those of you who missed our earlier news bulletins on this sensational daylight raid, here again are the main details. The woman entered the bank and was interviewed in the manager's private office. We have as yet no information on what took place at the interview. The Gorman Brothers Circus was parading through town, as three cowboys entered the bank. They held up the staff while the woman, evidently familiar with the security system, prevented manager Walter T. Penrose from taking action. Before leaving with the money, the bandits fired gas pellets which knocked out Penrose and the tellers, then triggered off the security system which sealed every exit from the premises. They then walked away in full view of the crowds watching the parade, and got into a small red convertible in a side street. Current police thinking is that the gang were picked up either by a helicopter or light airplane somewhere along the desert highway. The money? Well, it hasn't yet been possible for an accurate check to be made, but preliminary counts indicate that close to two hundred thousand dollars was stolen. President Arnold Carmody collapsed when he heard the news and your reporter — '

'What did he say?' demanded Tip thickly.

Benedict eased his weight off the cushion and rested it on his knees.

'How do you mean?' queried Jerry.

'About the dough. He said two hundred grand didn't he?'

'So?' asked Jerry innocently.

'So what am I getting? Pushed around, maybe?'

Tip's tone took on an evil edge.

'Something eating you, sonny?'

Benedict spoke softly, and an older hand would have identified the menace behind the words. So might Tip Brennan in the ordinary run of things. But now he was angry, the rage welling up inside and preventing him from reasoning clearly. Slowly, his voice thick, he said:

300

'I'm talking plain enough, *Mister* Benedict — '

Benedict, thought Jerry. Well now, that was something else new.

' — plain enough. The man said two hundred g's and I want to know what my end is.'

'You know what your end is,' Benedict replied. 'We talked about it at the start.'

'Talked about it?' Tip hooted. 'We didn't talk about nothing. You said that's what the job paid, and I listened. What was to talk? But now we got something to talk about. My cut.'

'Your cut, sonny, will be what I said, and what you agreed.'

It wasn't the words themselves that riled Tip so much, it was Benedict's calm assurance as he spoke them.

'Now you listen to me, big shot,' he shouted. 'All that cool bit, that's out. You wanta talk to me, talk like I'm as good as you. Because I am.'

He glared at the big man who watched the outburst unmoved.

'Hold on, kid,' pleaded Jerry, 'Listen,

no offence, but you don't know how these things run.'

Tip swung round. He'd forgotten Jerry for the moment, and that had been careless. After all, he didn't know where the old-timer stood, and now was the time to find out. Trying to keep his voice calm, he said:

'All right, man. Tell me how the thing runs.'

Jerry nodded vigorously, anxious to smooth things over.

'Now, first off, this dough. The guy on the radio, he said two hundred grand, right?'

'Right in one.'

'Sure, sure,' Jerry continued reasonably. 'Now this is an old cop trick. They put it out there's more money missing than the boys have got. Then they start picking on each other, thinking they're getting a shakedown from somebody. That's one thing.'

'Nuts to that,' growled Tip. 'The money's right there. All we have to do is count it. We don't have to take nobody's word.'

'O.K., O.K.' Jerry hurried on. 'Sure, you're right. Still, that is one thing. Then you have to remember the fix.'

'Fix?' queried Tip, 'Nobody never mentioned any fix to me.'

'Sure they didn't, but a big thing like this, there's a fix,' assured the older man. 'Ain't that right, Mr. Walker?'

Walker? thought Tip. Well, now we were getting somewhere.

'That's right,' confirmed the big man. 'But he don't want it from me. You tell him, Jerry. You're doing all right.'

Jerry nodded again, pleased.

'Nobody ever pulled anything this big without the fix going in. Maybe a quarter of the take, maybe a third. Either way, a big piece of change.'

Tip stared at him in disbelief.

'What are you trying to pull?' he snorted. 'That much of a cut? For that you could buy your own town.'

'Sometimes you have to buy half the town before you can operate,' nodded Jerry wisely.

Tip wrinkled up his brow with the effort of thinking.

'Suppose I believe you?' he demanded. 'The fix would work out around sixty-seventy thousand. I'm still not satisfied with the split.'

Benedict stood up quickly. The others tensed, ready for trouble.

'Before we waste any more time arguing, let's count it. That way, we'll know what it is we're arguing about.'

Tip was inflated. He'd made this guy sit up and beg all right. All that sonny bit, who did he think he was talking to? Just the same, it wouldn't do to turn his back on this guy, the way things stood. Benedict looked at him contemptuously, then turned his back towards him. Tip's fingers itched to pull the revolver from his waistband and get it over with. Jerry shook his head warningly. He couldn't see what all the fuss was about. Everything was all right. They had the dough, nobody had got hurt, all they had to do was lie low a few days. Everybody would get what he was promised, if only this fool kid would stop shouting around. In the old days he'd have put a slug in this punk himself. It was arguments like these that always worked out to the cops advantage in the end. But that was the old days. People didn't work that way anymore. Now it was smooth, all greased wheels and smooth like today. Why didn't the kid shut up?

'Count it,' commanded Benedict. 'You wanted to know how much there was. Count it.'

Tip shrugged and began opening one of the bags. Jerry helped him in silence. They began counting, stacking, counting again. Benedict sat, smoking quietly and watching. The minutes went by. Tip flung down a pile of bills and turned to him.

'This'll take forever,' he snapped. 'Can't you give a hand here?'

The big man shrugged.

'What for? I'm not interested. After you all get yours, what's left is mine. All of it. I'll count it later.'

'Yeah? We'll see about that.'

Furiously, Tip began counting again. The bills began to stack neatly on the table. Soon it was necessary to place a second layer on top of the first. The two men were absorbed in the work, eyes glistening as one thousand followed another.

Outside, Toni was becoming agitated. What was going on in there? Then an unpleasant thought went through her mind like a cold douche. There was another way out, a way she didn't know. They were gone, and the money too. She was being left to sit here and rot until the police came looking. Of course. That would be why she was still wearing this damned wig. She'd never explain that away. Once planted, the thought grew and expanded till she could think of nothing else. A patsy. She was being left behind. Well that might be what they thought. Snapping open her bag, she pulled out the little gun. That was something Benedict should have thought of. Shouldn't have left her the gun. Unless he'd figured she was so dumb it would be too late for her to do anything with it, by the time she'd worked out the score. That had to be it. They'd dumped her, those rats. It would explain many things. Not least it would account for none of them looking at her when they came out to collect the bags. She climbed out of the car and walked towards the stairs.

'One hundred sixty seven thousand, and a few bills,' announced Tip.

''Bout what I get,' agreed Jerry.

Benedict said nothing, but looked from one to the other.

'I don't know what you told these others, but my cut ain't big enough.'

Tip narrowed his eyes and spoke the words quietly. Jerry stepped a pace backwards. Without looking at him, Benedict addressed Jerry.

'And what about you? Any squawks?'

Jerry shook his head rapidly.

'No. Long as I get what you promised, I'll keep my end of the deal.'

'Don't be a sucker,' whispered Tip. 'This guy is walking off with all the gravy. What we get is carefare.'

Benedict waited to see whether Jerry would have anything to say. When the little man kept quiet, he said gently:

'So it looks as though you're on your own, punk. And I tell you this. You'll take what's yours and get out now, or your share is nothing. No dollars, no cents. Well?'

Tip hesitated. The big guy was tricky, he knew that. This was no time for grandstanding. He had to be tricky too. Sighing, he heaved his shoulders.

'If nobody's backing me, I guess that's it. O.K. to take mine and blow?'

'Go ahead,' Benedict told him.

Tip turned back to the table, the front of his body hidden from the seated man. He began to gather stacks of bills. When there were twenty on the pile, he looked round at Benedict.

'You wanta count 'em?'

'Why not?' agreed the big man.

Tip piled the thin stacks in his left hand and began to turn. As he did so, his hidden right hand pulled the heavy revolver from his waistband.

'Count 'em sucker,' he snarled, hand tightening on the trigger.

The cushion in Benedict's hand jumped twice. There were muffled thuds as the first slug hit Tip in the chest and the second smashed into his throat. His shout of pain became a strangled gurgle as blood spurted in a fountain from his severed jugular. Convulsively, his finger squeezed on the trigger once, then again. The noise of the heavy weapon crashed deafeningly in the small room, then it fell from a nerveless hand.

Jerry screamed and grabbed at his middle, blood oozing thickly between the clutching fingers. Tip had fallen backwards against the money table. Feeling support against his back, he rolled sideways and lay across the table, clawing at the surface to keep him upright. Great waves of redness passed over his eyes. Why couldn't he hold something? His hands seemed to be sliding all over the place. His knees gave way and slowly he sank down.

As he crumpled, his hands were pulling stacks of bills to the floor. Jerry was swaying to and fro, breathing heavily, a look of shocked disbelief on his face.

'What a break,' he croaked. 'What a lousy break.'

Benedict said nothing. His mind was filled with thoughts of how to meet the emergency. No one would have heard his own gun, wrapped in the cushion as it was, but there was a good chance somebody could have heard the other gun. One thing was certain, he couldn't stay here. There was another problem too. What to do about Jerry. He would die eventually, Benedict had no doubt about that. He'd seen too many guys with holes in their middles not to know what the final outcome would be. But that was eventually. It may take days. And in days policemen could get a lot of information from a dying man. It seemed a pity, but Jerry alive was too big a risk to take.

There was a crash as Tip Brennan hit the floor, pulling a shower of bills after him. Dying, he was dying. It didn't seem possible it could be happening to him.

Outside, Toni heard the two shots and stopped. So they hadn't gone at all. Instead they were fighting. Now she was afraid. Two shots could mean a lot of things. At the worst there could be two dead men in there, and that would still leave one. One who had killed twice and was unlikely to be merciful to the one person who could place him square in the gas chamber. As the thought struck her she ran for the big doors behind her. Locked. Looking around desperately, she raced to the nearest car and crouched down behind it, watching the wooden steps.

Jerry's face was ashen now. Benedict watched him curiously. If this one was going to die without any help, so much the better. The thing now was to get moving. He put away the gun and dragged an empty suitcase from behind the divan. Stepping over Tip's corpse he went to the table and began packing the money away. His fingers touched wetness and he looked with distaste at the stack splashed with Brennan's blood. Behind him, Jerry's lips were moving.

'Help me,' but there was no sound. 'Get a doctor. I'm bleeding to death. Help me.'

The light was fading in the room, and Jerry knew it wasn't the daylight going. It was the darkness of death. What a lousy break. All over that punk kid. And this guy, this Walker he was going to take off and leave him to die. Just like that.

There was no more room in the case. Benedict snapped the catches down, and looked at Jerry. The little man was resting against the wall now. Benedict had seen many men die, and he knew this one would not be long. He waved his hand briefly.

'So long, pal. Tough break you got there.'

'You — you can't — '

It took all Jerry's strength to squeeze out the words, but he couldn't get any further. Benedict grinned.

'Watch me.'

⋆   ⋆   ⋆

The beat officer listened to the agitated woman who'd rushed up to him.

'Shots, lady?'

Plenty of people had started drinking early today, but this woman didn't seem the kind. Still, shots?

'Two of them officer, very loud and not far off.'

'Well, we'll look into it, lady. I'll report in.'

She grabbed at his arm.

'You'll do something, and right now. I have two children in the house, and I want action. Tell you something else, I've done plenty hunting in my time and I know a gun when I hear one.'

He paused and scratched his chin. Could be. The whole town was crazy today anyhow, what with the bank raiders getting clean away and all. Why not a little shooting, too? Ah, there was a patrol car. He could see what they thought. As he waved, the cruiser nosed towards the kerb and a young man with tow-coloured hair stuck his head out.

'What's up, Mack?'

'This lady says she heard some shots.'

'Two of them,' she repeated. 'And very near by.'

'Shots?' echoed the patrol man incredulously. 'On Nelson Street?'

'I never heard tell of a gun asking what street it was on before somebody fired it,' she sniffed.

The tow head withdrew from sight.

'Better call in, Sid,' he advised. 'That lady swears she heard some shooting.'

313

He waited for his partner to chuckle, but he didn't. Instead he picked up the hand microphone and began to talk rapidly.

'Car One Seven on Nelson,' he intoned. 'Report of shooting in the area. This could be it. Maybe those guys never left town. Instruct immediately.'

'Wait, One Seven.'

The younger man looked at him in wonder.

'You mean you think this could be those mugs from the bank? But they're clear of town. It was on the radio.'

His partner nodded grimly.

'I have ears. But nobody's seen 'em since. And this is a shooting report. What's that?'

A fat man came bustling along, clad in a dirty under-shirt. Not the attire for Nelson Street.

'Officer, officer,' he panted 'You gotta come quick. There's been shooting.'

The woman looked triumphantly at the officer on the beat.

'You see?'

'Yes ma'am.'

He leaned in at the car window.

'This man heard it too,' he reported. 'You gonna call in?'

'Already have,' he was told. 'Just waiting for the word.' The microphone crackled.

'One Seven, this is Chief Lindsay. Repeat your message.'

The patrol car officer repeated it.

'Very well. I'm assuming the worst here. Remain where you are. I'm going to seal off that entire block. Meantime, if you see anybody acting suspiciously, you know what to do. But no guns unless you're driven to it. We can't be sure yet. Understood, One Seven?'

'Got it chief.'

The two officers got out of the car, each undoing the flap on his brown leather holster.

'There's help coming, lady. Now tell us the whole thing from the beginning.'

★   ★   ★

At the wooden steps, Benedict paused. He didn't like what he was going to do.

He never liked to harm a woman if he could help it, and this one had got under his skin a little. But only a lunatic would leave her alive after what had happened in the room behind him.

Toni watched him emerge, her heart thumping with excited fear. The little gun was in her hand, and she wasn't going to be taken so easily if she could help it. Benedict walked to the car where he'd left her, peered in and made a sound of annoyance. Might have known he couldn't rely on her just waiting there after those shots. Still, she couldn't get out. The key of the big doors was in his pocket. Time was important though. He'd have to find her fast. Putting down the case, he took out his gun and hefted it. Toni shrank back as far as she could behind the protection of the car. Benedict, uncertain where to begin, walked to the nearest vehicle and peered inside. Then he looked underneath. He'd be able to check the whole place in two or three minutes. If he had two or three minutes.

* * *

Chief Lindsay stalked busily from his car to the waiting officers.

'All right, let's have it quick,' he snapped.

They told him what they'd been able to learn from witnesses. He paid careful attention, squinting along the block as he listened.

'That makes it between Carver and Moon Lane, yes?' he queried.

'That's about what we made it, chief,' agreed Sid.

The chief walked away and talked into a microphone handed to him by his driver. Then he came back.

'The area will be shut down tight in two minutes,' he said. 'If this is what I'm betting it is, you men won't regret this day's work.'

They all nodded at one another, pleased. From far off, a siren wailed its mournful tune.

'What the hell,' roared the chief. 'I gave strict orders — '

As though his voice had carried, the noise stopped immediately. Black patrol cars began to nose into view from all directions.

★   ★   ★

Benedict pricked up his ears. That was a siren all right. Could be anything, any routine police emergency. Could be, but after those shots he couldn't take the chance. He'd have to leave the girl after all.

'You,' he shouted. 'Your cut is inside. I'm leaving. If you get caught, don't squeal on me, or you'll be dead before you reach a courtroom. Get your money and beat it.'

Lousy. A lousy way to end such a beautiful caper. If it hadn't been for that kid — . He dashed to the car and flung the money inside. Keys. Keys. Running to the big doors he unlocked them and flung them open. Quickly back to the car, inside, and the sweet sound of the motor. Maybe the girl would get away. Better for him if she did. Not that they'd catch up with him even if she talked. Out through the doors into the sunlit street. What was that car parked at the end?

The men in the patrol car watched the convertible as it came towards them.

Wrong make, wrong colour. And only one man inside. Still, the chief said nobody out.

Benedict swore as the two policemen drew guns and waved him down. He might kill these two and get past, but this was a cordon. He couldn't fight the whole department.

'Little trouble, officer?' he enquired innocently. 'And there's no need for those weapons, you know. I'm not a spy.'

The nearest man nodded, but didn't lower the gun.

'Sorry to trouble you, mister. Emergency cordon. Mind if we look over the car?'

'Certainly. Why not?'

Benedict got out, smiling broadly. He might even fool these clowns.

'Going on a vacation?'

The officer pointed to the case.

'Oh no, no. Just a few samples,' he replied easily. 'I'm a travelling man.'

'Uh huh.' The cop seemed satisfied. 'Mind if we take a look?'

'No, never refuse a sale.'

Benedict walked forward jauntily and

reached for the case.

'Ah, never mind. I guess it's O.K.'

His hand on the nearest catch, Benedict relaxed and drew back. The policeman leaned back inside. There was something on the floor in the rear. A hat? No, not a hat. A wig, a grey wig. He pulled it clear and held it out.

'This what you sell, mister? Theatrical stuff?'

'Why, yes — among other things.'

'Just a minute.'

The other cop came and stared at the wig in his partner's hand.

'It was a dame with grey hair with that mob at the bank this morning. This could be a coincidence, but I don't like coincidences.'

The gun, slack in his hand, came up fast and pointed steadily at Benedict's middle.

'Now I think we take a look at the samples.'

* * *

Toni almost cried out with relief when Benedict shouted at her. Just in time she prevented herself. It didn't take long to put a bullet in somebody, and she was certain that was what he would do if he found her. Then the car drove out of the big doors and he was gone. She waited, listening intently. She wouldn't put it past him to stop outside, then creep back to see if she'd come out of her hiding place. But the car went away up the street.

She sighed heavily and stood upright. The money. He'd said the money was up there. With them. With the other two, the ones he'd killed. It wouldn't be pretty, but she had to have that money. Bracing herself she walked quickly across to the wooden steps, which creaked noisily as she went up. The first room was empty. They must be in the rear, through that door.

Jerry lay on the floor. He'd kept his end, done all he had to do. Now he was here dying, while that rotten fourflusher walked away with the pot. He knew he was dying, but grimly he hung on to the last shreds of life. His mind was filled with a black hatred. Hatred for that dead punk lying a few feet away. But above all, hatred for the big man. The one who forced him into this, then walked out while he was dying. Was that a noise? The steps, somebody was coming up the steps. Maybe he was coming back for the rest of the dough. Tip's revolver lay a few inches from his hand. Painfully he stretched out an arm, fingers closing over the familiar cold of the butt. If it was him, Jerry would get him. His last act on this earth, but the one he'd have chosen anyway. Or cops maybe. It made no difference. To take one more uniform with him would be a good end too. The gun was heavy, very heavy. Slowly he brought it up from the floor.

Toni hesitated. It would be grim in there, she knew. But she'd come this far, done those things for the money. And the money was in there, where they were. Gritting her teeth, she pushed open the door. There was a loud crash. Then pain. Pain in her chest, awful, crushing, final. She staggered, gripped at the door.

Jerry grinned. He couldn't see who it was, but he'd got him all right. Then his throat rattled and he died.

Toni stared at the hand she'd put to her

breast. Blood. Must have been shot, she thought, unbelieving. Shot. But who'd — ? The money. Get the money, think about this later. Couldn't move her feet. Ridiculous. And why wasn't there any light in the place. She was going to fall down. No, no. Get the money. Couldn't see it. They must have hidden it. Poor baby. Why d'you leave home that way. Bet you didn't always work in a place like this. I could do plenty for a babe like you. If I get that money I can get Rufe out of jail. Little brother Rufey. Nice curly hair. Never really meant any harm. Just wild that's all. There's no pain now. Just everything nice and warm. That's all a girl wants really. Little comfort and warmth. I could have been in pictures one time. Regular movies. Can't get up. Don't want to. Nice down here. Nice in the warm dark. The dark.

All dark now.

Dark.

We do hope that you have enjoyed reading this large print book.

Did you know that all of our titles are available for purchase?

We publish a wide range of high quality large print books including:
Romances, Mysteries, Classics
General Fiction
Non Fiction and Westerns

Special interest titles available in large print are:
The Little Oxford Dictionary
Music Book, Song Book
Hymn Book, Service Book

Also available from us courtesy of Oxford University Press:
Young Readers' Dictionary
(large print edition)
Young Readers' Thesaurus
(large print edition)

For further information or a free brochure, please contact us at:
Ulverscroft Large Print Books Ltd.,
The Green, Bradgate Road, Anstey,
Leicester, LE7 7FU, England.
Tel: (00 44) **0116 236 4325**
Fax: (00 44) **0116 234 0205**

THREE DAYS TO LIVE

Robert Charles

Mike Harrigan was scar-faced, a drifter, and something of a woman-hater. With his partner Dan Barton he searched the upper reaches of the Rio Negro in the treacherous rain forests of Brazil, lured by a fortune in uncut emeralds. Behind them rode three killers who believed that they had already found the precious stones. And then fate handed Harrigan not emeralds, but the lives of women, three of them nuns, and trapped them all in a vast series of underground caverns.

DEATH IN RETREAT

George Douglas

On a day of retreat for clergy at Overdale House, a resident guest, Martin Pender, is foully murdered. The primary task of the Regional Homicide Squad is to track down the bogus parson who joined the retreat. Subsequent events show that serious political motives lie behind the killing, but the basic lead to it all is missing. Then, three young tearaways corner the killer in the woods, and a chess problem, set out on a board, yields vital evidence.

MIX ME A MURDER

Leo Grex

A drugged girl, a crook with a secret, a doctor with a dubious past, and murder during a shooting affray — described as a 'duel' by the Press — become part of a developing mystery in which a concealed denouement is unravelled only when the last danger threatens. Even then, the drama becomes a race against time and death when Detective Chief Superintendent Gary Bull insists on playing his key role of hostage to danger.

DEAD END IN MAYFAIR

Leonard Gribble

In another Yard case for Commander Anthony Slade, there is blackmail at London's latest night spot. Ruth Graham, a journalist, and Stephen Blaine, a blackmail victim, pit their wits against unusual odds when sudden violence erupts. Then Slade has to direct the 'Met' in a gruelling bout of police work, which involves a drugs gang and a titled mastermind who has developed blackmail into a lucrative practice. The climax to the case is both startling and brutal.